ROUGH EDGE

The Edge - Book One

CD REISS

Rough Edge
CD Reiss
The Edge - Book One
ISBN: 9781718830844
© 2018 Flip City Media Inc.
All rights reserved.

If any person or event in this book seems too real to be true, it's luck, happy coincidence, or wish-fulfillment on the reader's part.

AUTHOR'S NOTE: I did research. A ton of it. But I also make stuff up for a living.

There are a thousand ways to break something and more than one method of repair. Institutions we think we know from experience have engaged thousands of others in their own, equally valid experiences. What you assume is an error may be something else entirely. Or I might have fucked up.

You can poke me with corrections on any number of subjects and if I can fix an error, I will. I'm wrong a lot.

Also, liberties were taken.

Part One

HOMECOMING

Chapter One

GREYSON
NEW YORK CITY
NOVEMBER - 2006

He was a son of a bitch, a cold-hearted compartmentalizer with a heart of solid stone. His hands were instruments of brutal precision, and his cock was a means of punishment.

He wasn't the man I'd married, but he was my husband.

I couldn't see him, even though he was kneeling between my legs. My jaw was pushed back so far, I could only see out the window next to the bed. Two fingers were jammed in my mouth. His other hand was inside my knee, pressing it to the mattress until my legs were open as far as they could go.

"Suck," he commanded with a voice drained of emotion. A flat order, like "sit" or "heel."

I curved my lips around the fingers and sucked on them. They tasted of rubbing alcohol and pussy.

"Harder."

I sucked harder and he pushed my jaw up, restraining me with my position. He ran his other hand from my knee to the inside of my thigh. When he got to the fleshiest part, he tightened his grip until pain blossomed under his fingers and grew outward, lacing my arousal with its companion—pain.

When he let go, I whimpered around his fingers, and he responded by pushing them deeper down my throat. As he leaned over me, I felt his rod of an erection where I was wet.

He whispered into my cheek, "Take them. All the way." I opened my throat and he pushed his fingers down. "Beg for it."

I couldn't speak with his fingers in my mouth. I couldn't even breathe.

"You're not begging." His fingers were down to the webs and my body contracted around them for air. He pulled them out. "Beg."

"Fuck me. Please fuck me."

"What?" With his spit-soaked hand, he reached between my legs and pinched my swollen clit.

"Put your cock in me. Fuck me hard. Take what you want. Please. Please." The last word came as a whisper.

He got on his knees, magnificent, cut like a god from jaw to abs to the hard heat of his thighs. One hand on my sternum to hold me still, the other guiding his cock between my legs. I was so wet, open like a hungry flower, still whispering *please please please* as he leaned his weight on my chest and drove into me. He was long and thick. Without prep, he could hurt me, and he did.

I knew when to look for the change. I knew how to see him recover himself in the violence. In the moment he drove through me so hard he cracked, went supple, and became my husband again.

The first orgasm came on the third thrust and lasted until he joined me in heaven.

GREYSON
FORT BRAGG
AUGUST - 1992

BASIC TRAINING WAS A CAKEWALK. Last course. Blue group did belly robber, high step over, low wire, weaver, and island hopper. Halfway through, I fell fifteen feet off the confidence climb. I thought I'd wiped out for good with my full weight on my right wrist and the rest of the blue group's boots smacking the mud all around me.

"Get up, you little fucking shit!"

Ronin.

That was Ronin yelling, and Ronin grabbing me under the

arms to throw me toward the next obstacle.

"Move it!" He pushed me. "I'm staying behind you, so if you go pussy, you're answering to me!"

I tucked my wrist under my breasts, dropped to my knees and crawled under the low wire. He was behind me, shouting a litany of encouragements and insults. I climbed the wall with one hand and my teeth and stumbled over the line in the middle of the pack, aching, bruised, tears streaking the mud on my face. Ronin was at attention behind me.

"That doesn't look like attention, Frazier!" Sergeant Bell shouted.

I put my right arm to my side and straightened my wrist. Pain shot through to my shoulder, but still, I stood at attention. Bell didn't seem satisfied.

"You're up shit creek now, Private One More."

"Fuck you, Ronin."

Bell stormed to me, hands clasped behind his back, nearly crashing into Rodrigo, who was trying to get into the line. Rodrigo buckled and found his space. Bell was not deterred. I put my eyes at attention and tried to tamp down the heavy breaths. Everything hurt. I felt as if I'd flung myself out of a moving car, but I stood still.

When Bell got uncomfortably close, I expected him to shout, but he murmured two words so low, only I could hear them.

"Stop smiling."

Chapter Two

The sky in Iraq was the bluest blue I'd ever seen. It had a flat depth, as if thin layers of glass, each a slightly different shade, were stacked together. Sometimes I'd dream about that sky. Either I'd be floating in it, blue everywhere, above and below, at each side and pressure point, squeezing the breath out of me, or I'd be falling from it, from blue into blue, no Earth barreling into greater and greater detail. Just a single direction in the never-ending cerulean sky.

Caden and I had been separated by an ocean and a war for ten months. We'd married while I was on leave and spoke when our schedules matched and the wind blew the wi-fi signal in the right direction. I thought I hadn't known him long enough to miss him, but I did.

Painfully. Tenderly. Thoroughly. Our separation stretched the bond between us to a thin, translucent strand, but did not break it.

Caden's eyes had the color and layered depth of the Iraqi sky.

When I missed him, I looked up. When I wrapped his T-shirt around my neck, my dreams of the blue sky lost their nightmarish edge, and the bond became a little less taut.

Jenn and I flew to New York in our uniforms. She remained on active duty and had a job waiting at the VA Hospital in Newark. I had a husband and no job.

"You want to put on some makeup or something?" she asked.

"Why? You afraid they're all looking at me?"

The crew had moved us to first class. I craned my neck to see a jowly businessman sleeping with his mouth open. A mid-level rap star with cornrows and a name I couldn't recall was reading a book to his daughter, and two middle-aged women chatted in the row across. No one was giving my lashes the side-eye.

"Hell, no. But maybe you want to look nice for your husband?" She rooted around a quilted pink bag and found a black stick. "Here. Lip gloss."

"It's only going to wind up on his dick."

She burst out laughing and replaced the lip gloss with mascara. "Here. Doll it up just a little. You're a civilian now."

I took the mascara, and she handed me a compact with a mirror. I flipped it open and looked at myself in circular sections.

I was a civilian now.

I had no idea how to be that.

AS THE ONLY girl in a military family, enlisting wasn't encouraged. It wasn't unexpected either. It made them proud. And disappointed. And worried. A mixed bag of emotions that probably had nothing to do with either parent and everything with how I felt at every time I wondered what they thought.

I would have stayed in the army my entire life, but Caden happened, and he saw the army as his duty to the country. A debt to pay, not a way of life.

At the gate, a little girl of about six ran up and gave Jenn and me flowers. "Thank you for your service," she said.

This wasn't uncommon. I'd learned people were in awe of my career choice and the risks it involved.

I kneeled and took the flowers. "Thank you for the flowers. And thank you for appreciating us. That means a lot."

Suddenly shy, she curtsied and ran away to her mother, who waved at me. I gave her a thumbs-up.

"Is it wrong to wish she was a single, six foot-tall black man with a nice bank account?" Jenn asked quietly, sniffing the flowers.

"Her mother might be a little surprised."

Jenn chuckled and pointed at the sign above. "Baggage claim, this way."

We didn't get two steps before I saw Caden waiting for me. He had flowers tied with stars and stripes printed on the ribbon, a grey suit, and smile that told me he saw me the way I saw him—with a certain amount of surprise at the easy familiarity, and another bit of gratitude at the fulfilled expectations. It was as if we were seeing each other for the first time, and coming back to something very familiar.

I dropped my bag and ran into his arms. We clung to each other, connected in a kiss that held nothing back. Cocooned, shielded by love and commitment, the airport terminal fell behind the wall of our attention to the kiss.

He jerked me away with a sucking sound and a drawn breath, but kept his nose astride mine. "Welcome to New York, Major."

That was when I heard the applause.

"Are we making a spectacle of ourselves?" I let my body relax away from his.

"I fucking love you so much, I don't even care."

I looked at the people surrounding us. I was in camo and he had a flag ribbon on the flowers. We were indeed making a spectacle of ourselves.

Jenn dropped my bag at my feet. "That was so sweet I almost clapped."

Caden took it before I could. "Thank you for not."

The crowd dispersed, and we headed out of baggage claim without further incident.

———

"WHAT DO you want to see first?" Caden asked after we dropped Jenn off at her parents' brownstone in Fort Greene. His wrist was draped over the steering wheel of his Mercedes. The band of his expensive watch caught glints of the sun. The seats were soft black leather. There was no dust or sand on the carpets, and none of the upholstery was torn.

"The inside of my eyelids."

"Come on, Major. Push on." He squeezed my knee and kissed me at the red light. "You'll sleep when you're dead."

I put my hand over his, and he stroked my thumb. "Were your eyes always this blue?"

"Probably."

They looked bluer against the New York sky, which was fluffed with late summer clouds. I sat back and looked out the window. Maybe tomorrow I'd see the color I'd fall through.

"What are my choices?" I asked.

"The house, your new office, or any restaurant in the city."

That was more choices than I was used to, and none involved getting sand in the crack of my ass or telling a man it was okay to kill people.

"Can we eat in?"

"Yep."

The seams in the bridge's surface went *puh-puh-puh* under the tires and the web of cables holding it up blurred in my peripheral vision. Manhattan stretched ahead of me like a dense construction of grey bricks. I didn't know where people fit into such compactness.

"Okay," I finally said. "The house."

CADEN PUT the car in a garage a block away. Apparently he'd bought the spot years ago. It required a mortgage and operating fees. Where I grew up, you parked in a lot someone else owned, your own driveway, or on the street.

This was my new normal.

On the walk along Columbus Avenue, I felt as if I were wearing a camo clown suit. Caden put his arm around me and kissed my temple as we waited at the light. The crowd crossed before the light changed to green, but I followed my husband.

"We're on 87th between Columbus and Amsterdam," he said. "Avenues run north-south, streets run east-west."

"Got it." We turned onto a narrow, tree-lined street. "This is a nice block."

"It is."

The houses were stone and connected to each other on the sides. Some were slightly set back from the street to accommodate a stoop and a few steps down to a garden apartment.

He stopped by one such house and held his hand out while the other took my duffel off his shoulder. "Here we are."

I looked up. Garden apartment. Three stories. An attic with stone carvings around the leaded windows. "Is it all yours?"

He threw the duffel up the steps. It made it halfway. "It's all ours."

He picked me up in his arms before carrying me up the stoop. I squeaked in surprise. We laughed as he tried to unlock the door without dropping me, and when he managed to do it, I cheered.

He retrieved my bag and dropped it in the foyer. We were at the base of a flight of stairs. Everything was polished dark wood carved at the corners. A beveled mirror was set into a frame with three brass hooks under it. I took off my cap and let my hair fall.

I was fully overwhelmed. He took my cap and put it on a hook before taking my face in his hands and kissing me.

"I have your back," he whispered. "Okay?" I nodded, and he kissed me again. "Say it for me."

"You have my back."

"And your front."

I smiled into his kiss. "You have my front."

"I can take you to the bedroom if you insist or on the stairs right now."

"Will you give me a minute to shower?"

"You have rank."

"That's an order then."

He got his hips under me and his hands under my ass, hitching me up until I could get my legs around his waist. He carried me to our room. I didn't see anything but his face on the way up. I only knew there were wood floors and windows. Two flights. A tower with me on top.

HE SAT me on a bench in the bathroom and turned the water on in the white claw-foot tub. He kneeled in front of me to unlace my boots. I couldn't stop looking at him in his fancy suit, kneeling on the bathroom floor to service me.

"I hate that they make us wear this shit on the way home," he said. "It's total PR."

"Yeah, well, the military is nothing without its symbols, and that's what I am."

"Were." He pulled off the boot. "Now you are Dr. Greyson Frazier, MD, with a psychiatric practice in Manhattan." He peeled off my socks. "And my wife. Stand up."

Still on his knees, he undid my buckle and fly and pulled my pants down, letting his palms spread out over the skin of my thighs. I stepped out of them and he tossed the pants aside.

"Ah, I missed this." He lifted my shirt and kissed the silver scar over my heart. He kissed my belly and the triangle below. I put my fingers in his hair, and he reached up under my clothes until he found my hardened nipples.

"Caden," I groaned. "Bath."

With a gentle suck on my belly, he stood. I started unbuttoning from the top and he unbuttoned from the bottom. We met in the middle and got all my clothes off until I wasn't wearing anything but the dog tags that hung between my breasts.

He laid them in his palm and looked at them, letting one clink against the other.

"Take them off," I said.

He closed his fist around them and pulled them over my head. The chain slid against my long, straight hair, and I was free.

Caden coiled the chain on the vanity. I shut off the water and tested it.

Scalding hot.

No one in the world knew me the way he did.

HE'D TAKEN his jacket off, rolled up his sleeves, and bathed me, touching every part of my body. His hands knew exactly how to tease me. They were accurate and subtle, driving my desire forward without letting me come.

He tossed the towel away and threw me on the bed, soaking wet.

He didn't even undress to fuck me. Not right away. He just spread my legs and slid his fingers inside me, then took out his monster of a cock and fucked me as if we hadn't seen each other in four months.

The sheets were white.

The furniture was honey, and the lamps were Tiffany.

Day turned into evening, but the street didn't quiet.

That was all I noticed between orgasms.

In the darkness, we curled under the covers. He stroked my arm with his thumb, appreciating every inch of skin.

"I haven't shown you the house," he said. "I'm sorry."

"Are you going to show me all your childhood secret hiding places?"

"The speakeasy in the basement? Yes."

He'd told me about the Prohibition-era space the first owners had dug out of the basement. How it had false walls, a mosaic tile floor, a mahogany bar, and secret places to hide customers and almost a century later, small children.

"It's a really nice house," I said. "Is this a good neighborhood, as neighborhoods go in New York?"

"This block is unattainable."

"What's that mean?"

"This house is priceless. I could name a number and get it."

"Your dad was smart to buy it when he did."

"He wanted to be near enough to the hospital, but not that close. He had a space for a practice in the garden apartment, which is soon to be..." He waited for me to finish.

"My practice."

"Bingo."

"I'm nervous."

"I know."

"What if I—"

He put his finger on my lips before I could utter my litany of doubts. "You're going to do fine. And if it takes longer than you think it should, we can survive on a heart surgeon's salary for a while."

Of course we could. There was nothing to be nervous about. He had my back and my front.

"Can I see the office?"

"Yes."

WE WIGGLED into pajamas and went down the back stairs, which led to a short carpeted hall with an old wooden door at each end.

"The door at the back leads to a shared kind of alley thing out the front, so patients won't bump into each other on the way in and out," Caden said as he turned the skeleton key that stuck out of the office's keyhole. It clacked deeply before the door swung open. He flicked on the lights.

The office defied every expectation.

I expected cold fluorescents and a dropped ceiling.

What I got was a pristine white ceiling and warm lamps.

I expected an empty space.

What I got was a 1950s era desk and chairs, tufted couch, end tables, a clock where I could see it but the patient couldn't, and a deep blue carpet to muffle the distracting scrape of chairs and footsteps. Behind the desk, a horizontal filing cabinet had framed pictures leaning on the top. Family. Friends. Caden and me on the rooftop of the hotel in Amman, with the sunset behind us. I picked up our wedding photo. My parents had set up the backyard in flowers and tables, doing the best they could when they heard we were getting hitched on two-day leave. Caden and me outside the combat hospital in Balad, dressed in dull green and smiles.

"I read up on what you'd need. They said family pictures humanized you to patients."

"That's right."

He opened the door on the far end of the room. The waiting room was bathed in the same warm lamplight. It was small. Two chairs and a love seat. A coffee table. A Wasily Kandinski print. Everything matched the interior office.

"I had speakers put in." He pointed up. Small wood-grain boxes hung in the corners where the ceiling met the walls. "I hear music soothes the savage breast."

Caden, a psychiatrist's husband, had hang-ups about mental illness that had revealed themselves after I accepted his proposal.

"I won't be working with savages," I said with a raised eyebrow. I was going to have to patiently whittle away this particular neurosis.

"They won't all have breasts either." He put his arm around me. "So you like it?"

"I love it. Madly, deeply. I love it." I put my arms around his shoulders, and his snaked around my waist. "Thank you so much."

"There's so much we're going to do together." He kissed my neck. "We're going to build an entire life out of a war."

"That would be a miracle."

"First of many. You and me. We're a miracle." He pulled back so he could see my face. "You know what I see when I look at you?"

"Your wife?"

"The worst decisions I've ever made, I made for a reason. You. You rose out of the destruction. Our life together will be built into the best from what survived the worst."

"That's very poetic."

He smiled. "I've been thinking about what to say for days. I wanted to explain how magnificent we're going to be."

"Magnificent?"

"I don't think I quite nailed it." He took me back into the hall and to an unremarkable door under the stairs. "Basement."

He opened the door, and flicked on the light. Wooden stairs led to a dirt floor in a four-by-five room. Caden reached around me and put his hands on a vase sitting on a set-in shelf. He yanked it, and the wall slid to the side, revealing a mosaic floral floor and dark wood bar stacked high with cardboard boxes.

"Chez Columbus," he said, smiling. "1925-1933."

Amazing. An actual speakeasy with a stairway to the hidden alley on the side of the house, hidden rooms, and lastly, behind the laundry room, a big wall safe. He opened it, then pushed away the wall behind it to yet another room with cylindrical holes in the concrete.

"The bottle room," he said. "This was where I hid when... you know."

"When you were scared."

"When I should have been stopping him from beating her."

"I'm going to get you out of the habit of blaming yourself."

"Good luck." He held out his hand, moving the subject away from the abuse of his mother as he always did. "Come on. It's cold in here."

The steps to the bedroom seemed like an eternal climb, but we wound up racing to the top. It didn't matter who won. We both landed on the bed.

We held each other tight, and I felt safe starting a new life with him.

THAT NIGHT, with the *whoosh* of cars outside and a police siren whining far away, he woke with a grunt and a command. "Stop!"

I reached for my revolver, but it was locked away in a strange closet, in the strange bedroom, in a city that was a sea of stone.

But he was there, the street light blue on his cheek, and all was well as long as he was next to me.

"Caden? Are you okay?"

"Yeah." He rolled over to face me. "Sorry."

"What was it?"

"Dream. Nothing."

PTSD was as real as the war itself, and I had to know if he was reliving it in his sleep. "Caden. Can you tell me?"

"Pieces of me were breaking off."

"Were you in Iraq? In the dream?"

"No." His denial was barely a whisper.

I took it for a normal nightmare and joined him in sleep.

Chapter Three

CADEN

Greyson was back, and like good news when nothing's going right or a seat by the radiator after a day in the snow, she brought relief to pain I forgot I was feeling.

As soon as she agreed to marry me, while I was still deployed, I started getting the house ready. I met with an architect and contractor on a short leave, and again on the way back from our wedding in California. I was barely off the plane before I started furnishing the house. I had an attending position waiting at Mt. Sinai, but she had nothing and I needed to give her everything.

The house had been unoccupied since I left. Dad's office was a wreck. I'd had it ripped down to the studs. Had the shitty memories scraped out of the plaster and sanded off the wood. When I resigned my commission and returned, it was all details and new furniture.

That was when the dreams started.

Or more accurately, the dream. They were all the same dream, the way a woman was the same woman from all angles, naked or dressed. Same person, only time and situations changed.

I was somewhere in the house. The windows were painted over. I was in tremendous dream pain. Meaning I was terrified to the point of pain, but I couldn't physically feel my body being torn in two.

Obviously. It was just a dream. I never felt pain in my dreams.

The dreams weren't long. They came in the middle of the night, and I woke enraged, because I wasn't just coming apart. Something was taking me apart. It had to be stopped.

But when I woke to Greyson's voice, I wasn't pissed off at the dream thing. I was fine, and I went back to sleep. It hadn't come back in two nights.

"It's nice to not have to rush through surgery," I said, swinging my racquet at the tiny blue ball. It popped off the front wall, made it past the receiving line, and took off for the back wall.

Danny thought he was in an action movie, again, and tried to climb the wall to get it, managing to just get it back into play. I slammed it to the other side of the court while he was recovering.

"How about not getting shot at? Is that an improvement?" Danny said as I helped him up. He was a buddy from my residency at NYU Medical. Pediatric surgery, but he floated into general pediatrics when he didn't have the intestinal fortitude to cut into children.

"No one was shooting at me." I snapped up the ball and got ready for my serve. "It was easy."

"I still think it was stupid," he said. "But you lived, so whatever. They were your years to waste."

"Wouldn't have met Greyson."

I served. He was better set up this time and won the point.

"Yes! One more and drinks are on you, Private."

"Captain."

"You're nothing out here, buddy. What's Greyson? A major? That higher than captain?"

"Yes, but we're nothing here."

"Your woman still ranks you."

"Trash talk won't win you the point." I bounced the ball, setting up a serve that wouldn't overpower him, which he'd be ready for, but one to surprise him.

"That's right. I forgot you were unshakable."

I served. He was off guard, recovering enough to return but not win. Two points later, I had the game.

THE CLUB'S lounge wasn't crowded on weekdays. Out the floor-to-ceiling windows, the rooftops of Manhattan were laid out like a fallen dresser with drawers pulled out randomly.

Water towers, HVAC units, greenhouses, and patios dotted the rooftops, and through the slit of Second Avenue, I saw the southern tip of the island.

Danny placed our drinks on the table by the window and threw himself into the chair. Guy couldn't sit straight to save his life. I hadn't noticed that until I got back from my second deployment. Sloppiness had always bothered me, but slouching never had. All kinds of new things bugged me now, but more things seemed petty and unimportant. Status symbols. Expensive things. A woman everyone else wanted. None of that was interesting anymore.

"Sit up straight, would you?" I said. "You look like a rag doll."

"I'm entitled to sit like this today."

I tipped the Perrier bottle into the glass. The ice clicked. When it settled, I took a sip. "You blow one too many noses?"

"I had to refer a kid, thirteen... he was *thirteen*. Had to refer his parents to an oncologist they'll go broke paying. And it was hopeless. There was no... ah, never mind."

"Sorry, that's... well, it's part of the job. But sorry."

"Asshole." He crossed ankle over knee and drank his beer. He was a redhead and, in the ultimate irritating cliché, had a temper to match.

"I am an asshole."

"That some kind of opening for another war story?"

It hadn't been an opening any more than Dan's snide

comments were actual insults. My friend was making a request. He'd lost his brother on 9/11 and listening to me tell a war story made him feel as if he'd deployed with me.

"I had this guy on the table," I said. "We were low on morphine, so no one got it until we put them under, so he was screaming his head off. And rightfully so. His humerus was shattered."

"Very funny."

We clicked glasses, and I continued. "His arm was hanging on his body by half a bone. Rotator cuff was torn up. Skin had third-degree burns. I could put him back together well enough to get him to Baghdad, but it would have taken five hours. So meanwhile, you know what he's screaming?"

"Get the fuck on with the story?"

"'I'm a guitarist.'" I paused with my drink at my lips long enough to mutter, "He played fucking guitar." I put the glass down. "Meanwhile, they tell me there's another guy who's about to lose his leg. They clamped off the femoral artery, but it's going stiff real fast and he's going to need a graft."

"Who's triaging these people?"

"Someone who loves rock. But what do you do? You can save the arm or the leg. You can't save both. One gets a quick amputation. The other gets screws and pins. Which is it?"

"Do I get vitals?"

"Answer."

"Was either in shock?"

"This isn't a drill, Dan."

"Hang on—"

"There's no time."

"Jesus."

"Which?"

"All right, all right, asshole. What did you do?"

I finished my drink. "Decided it's easier to hold down a job with two legs and one arm than the other way around."

"You got something against music?"

"It was a calculation. Life over limb."

"You are one sick fuck." He put his elbows on his knees and shook his head in disappointment, but his smile told me he admired me. "How does your wife even deal with your shit?"

My wife had lived it with me, that was how.

"She didn't believe me. She came to Balad Base before the second Fallujah offensive to make sure we weren't fucked in the head. She wouldn't believe I could turn it on and off. She was like a pit bull, man."

She cared. More than her big brown eyes or the silken hair she kept twisted in a bun, I remembered her caring about my psychological well-being. I was no one to her, but she didn't want me to suffer. That first session, when I laughed at her, I also started to fall in love with her.

She hadn't believed that either. How could a man so detached feel love? How could I be brokenhearted one minute and perform surgery the next without opening myself to a crippling emotional breakdown?

Eventually, she learned I could do both. More than nimble hands and the will to finish med school, at-will detachment was my most valuable skill.

"I maintain going was stupid," Danny said. "Noble, but stupid."

"Like I said, I met Greyson."

"The internet works fine, thanks." He picked up his glass. "That's where I met Shari."

"When do I get to meet Shari? Or do I have to go on the internet to do it?"

"Soon. You want another?"

"Sure."

He went to the bar. The sky turned orange with the sunset.

You didn't meet women like Greyson on the internet. She'd spent her adult life in the army, and if she hadn't met me, she'd still be wearing boots and brown. She'd be fucking some other lifer.

She'd be living her life the way she always thought she would.

I'd rescued her from all that.

She'd be just fine.

Deployment after deployment. A slave to pay grade and rank. Stable.

Greyson wanted her boundaries pushed. She wasn't happy unless she was doing more, going faster, expanding in all directions. The military limited her ability to find how far she could go.

I hadn't considered that maybe the limits were the point.

When Dan came toward the table with the drinks, I resolved yet again to make sure Greyson was happy.

Chapter Four

GREYSON

I didn't just have to get used to New York or civilian life. I didn't just have to acclimate to finding work instead of having it given to me. I had to get used to being married.

Caden and I had met in a war zone. I'd been prepared to live in that zone my whole life. My family prized duty and loyalty to near fetish.

He had gotten a direct commission as a doctor in late 2001 out of a sense of duty he wasn't explicitly raised with. He held it in his heart next to his need to be a part of a solution. He entered the army with his privilege, his money, his medical pedigree, and a cockiness usually only found in fighter pilots and bomb specialists.

We were from different countries in the same America. When I'd arrived on base, he was just another good-looking soldier who wanted to get in my pants. Another one denying he was stressed. Too boastful, too proud, too full of himself to take no for an answer.

He broke down my professionalism by being honorable, dutiful, brilliant, and just enough of an asshole to remind me he was fully a man, and just vulnerable enough to remind me he was fully human.

He also smelled nice and had a casual way of touching me that made me want to purr.

My CO had issued me a pass just long enough to fly home and get married. We did it at my parents' house in San Diego. He had no one in New York. The night before we tied the knot, I had a vivid dream. In it, I was marrying the wrong man. On top of a tall building, guests filled the chairs. Mom congratulated me. Dad flew in on an F-14. Colin wore camo and boots he wouldn't be caught dead in outside a dream.

And I was marrying the wrong man. No one would listen. They thought I was crazy. I woke up in a terror, convinced I was making the mistake of my life.

Then I saw Caden sleeping next to me, and the terror fell away. I wasn't marrying the wrong man. I was marrying Caden, and he was *right*. I was never as sure about anything in my life as I was about him.

In New York, the last place on earth I thought I'd find myself, those first months of our relationship seemed like a dream. I remembered the blood, the explosions, the prayers uttered to a God I'd forgotten a hundred times, but the hours of gentle relief with him became more of a home base to balance against the violence I'd seen. That knowledge that no, I wasn't making bad decisions because he was with me, became my anchor.

Before we were married, and after he inadvertently rescued me from an assignment that would have ended my career, we both got approved for R&R.

We couldn't acknowledge each other on the streets of Amman, but in the American hotel, we could be a couple. We became intimate with the hotel tea shop and the details of our separate rooms. On the rooftop patio, he traced the red scar down my right wrist. His lips were parted a little, as if ready to kiss at any moment, and his face was lit by the sun's reflection.

"Your eyes match the sky," I said to him. His face was framed in the blue Iraqi ceiling.

"They're actually holes in my head," he said. "You're seeing right through."

Caden ran his fingers over the top of my hand, connecting the knuckles like a man taking territory one hill at a time. We were so deep inside each other, there was no such thing as a public place.

I hadn't gone to Iraq to fall in love. I was there to do the impossible—talk to soldiers about how they felt in a situation where feelings could kill. It was exhausting.

Caden energized me.

He traced the scars I'd gotten when I broke my wrist. "Does anyone think you tried to kill yourself?"

"Everyone. My mother still thinks I'm trying to hide a suicide attempt."

"Why?"

"I was a goth teen. Eyeliner out to here. The world was *so boring*, like, *so* uninteresting." I rolled my eyes dramatically.

"Can't imagine it." His fingers kept tracing the scar.

"I did want to... well, I almost gave up after I broke it. I lost flexibility, and it was permanent. I wanted to be a medic." The admission embarrassed me, because I'd failed.

"That doesn't surprise me at all." He lifted my face by the chin. "You're an adventurous spirit."

"So are you." I nudged him.

"No, really. You're pretty angry at your limitations."

"Angry?"

"Frustrated. Don't worry, we're going to get rid of either the anger or the limits."

"When?"

"Don't rush. We have a lifetime."

JENN SHOWED up in leggings and a gray army hoodie, exactly on time. Five in the morning like a good soldier. I was early, stretching on the summit of a huge boulder in Central Park. She joined me.

"Ronin's coming," she said. "That all right?"

Ronin and I had dated, if that was what you called sporadic sex in the first year of enlistment, then a long separation, then a few rolls in the hay when I was a resident at Walter Reed and he was working in Intelligence.

"What's he doing in New York?"

We took off down the boulder, stopped at a small rock embedded in the grass, and dropped for push-ups.

"Who knows?" Ten then back up the rock.

"Really?"

"Left Aberdeen Proving grounds." Top of the rock. Squat thrusts.

After everything that happened at Abu Ghraib, they'd sent him to Aberdeen. Jesus Christmas on a ladder, the army was fucked.

"They sent him here? Why?"

"He's out of uniform now."

Our breathing became unavailable for talking as we worked out. Ronin showed up midway through, in designer jeans and a sport jacket. He may have gone spook, but he was a handsome one. Dirty-blond hair, dark blue eyes in a face that had been chiseled and pristine when we met, but was wearing its ruggedness well.

"You doing it in that jacket?" I said between finishing push-ups and running back up the boulder.

"In a minute." He took out a cigarette and lit it.

Jenn gave him the finger. He waved.

I didn't think I could do another. The push-ups were murder on my wrist and my lungs burned.

"One more!" I cried, heading back down the boulder.

"I can't!" Jenn put her hands on her knees.

"You can!"

I was telling myself more than her. I pushed myself. Push-ups. Run. Squat thrusts. Run.

I fell to my knees on the grass and rolled onto my back.

Ronin slow-clapped with the cigarette dangling from his lips. "Nice work, Major One More."

Instead of telling him to go to hell, which would have taken a spare breath I didn't have, I held up my middle finger.

"Two from me!" Jenn held up both of her birds.

Ronin laughed and put his cigarette out under his shoe. "You're just jealous I don't have to work as hard as you." He picked up his cigarette butt and flicked it toward the garbage pail. It was too far to reach and too small a target, but it landed.

"What are you doing here, Ronin?" I asked.

Jenn put in her two cents. "Did Intelligence kick you out for lack thereof?"

He held his hands over his heart. "I'm wounded."

"No, really." I sat up. "I'm asking nice."

He shrugged. "Got an offer in the private sector."

Jenn and I both asked "Where?" at the same time.

"I can't say, and you both owe me a beer."

"Can't say?" I asked. "You were doing medical research."

"I still do. But, you know, it's still military shit. La-di-da." He broke a piece of grass and tossed it my way. "How's civilian life, Major? You adjusting?"

"Yeah. It's fine."

"She sucks at it," Jenn interjected.

"What's that supposed to mean?" I asked.

"You're still trying to impress the brass with one more lap."

"Shut up." I threw blades of grass at her, but she was right. I wasn't at home outside military life. Not yet.

"And the practice?" he asked. "How's it going?"

"She needs clients."

"Can I talk?" I kicked her gently.

"You're too slow."

"I could use some more clients."

"Said so."

We smiled at each other.

"Jenn here sent me a couple of guys from her art therapy group, and thank you."

"You're welcome."

"But that's only a couple."

"Most of my vets are from Jersey anyway," she added.

"Manhattan's tough," I agreed. "I specialized in battle trauma. They don't grow military here. They grow, I don't know, hedge fund managers and musicians."

"Yeah, here's the thing. How far are you going to push to do this?" Ronin asked, then continued before I could ask him what the fuck that was supposed to mean. "You're far outside your comfort zone here."

"I don't have a comfort zone."

"I'm asking if you're committed, Major One More."

"You know I am, Lieutenant Pain in the Ass."

"Good." He slapped his knees and stood as if we'd just ended a meeting. "I'll send you some people. See you around." He stepped away then turned back. "And Jenn?"

"What?"

He flipped her the bird and she laughed.

When he was out of earshot, she sighed. "Such a good-looking man with an ice-cold rock for a heart."

"Oh, not really. He had a heart once." I got my feet under me. "He never calls your rank."

"No, I guess not." I helped her up. "I never noticed."

"I think he likes you."

"I bet I can get to Columbus Station first."

"Hell, no."

And we were off for one more run.

Chapter Five

Greyson had been home three weeks the first time it happened. I was standing over a man with an empty chest. The pump kept his blood moving and the measured hiss of the ventilator told me he was breathing. We'd extracted a leg vein to replace the clogged artery.

I'd done this procedure at least a hundred times, and twice in an army hospital. I knew the rhythms of beeps and hisses. It was nothing. Vitals were good. Oxygen was good.

I held my hand out for the grafted vein. The nurse handed me the tray with the slice of flesh, and the whisper of the ventilator changed.

"What?" I said.

Everyone looked up. Pairs of dots of eyes over pale blue rectangles covering their mouths. Something was there with us, in the room, and it wanted me. If I'd been in a cave with a hungry lion, I'd be just as sure, except the lion didn't growl. It breathed in a throaty rattle with the shushing of the ventilator.

"What, what, Doctor?" Amy Sullivan, the assisting surgeon, asked.

I wasn't in a cave. There was no hungry lion. It was fine. The numbers were good. The ventilator was just...

"Can someone check the ventilator?"

"Ventilator checks out," the tech's voice came from behind me.

"You can tell that in two seconds? Can I have a swab, please?" I prepped for the graft. "Does it sound normal to you?" I said quietly to Amy.

"Yeah. Are you all right?"

I was sweating. My heart was racing. My adrenal glands were firing on all cylinders. This didn't happen to me. I always put the right feelings in the right boxes and slid the deadbolt closed until I needed them. I didn't make up stories, and I didn't hear voices in the equipment.

But the feeling of being besieged was as familiar as it was real, and I knew how to handle it.

This was war, and I could do my job in the middle of it.

"I'm fine. Let's put this guy's heart back in."

THE FEELING FOLLOWED me that night to our first anniversary dinner. When I saw her outside the restaurant, I kissed her and held her hand while we waited for our table. I decided not to ruin the evening. When I took her hand over the table and she tucked her foot between mine, I decided she didn't need to know at all. What was I supposed to say? "I was sure there was something but there wasn't?" Or, "Can you please diagnose me before bed?"

Being married to a psychiatrist had upsides. She prescribed sleeping pills when I needed them. In Fallujah, when I was in the field hospital OR for eight days without rest, she'd managed vitamins and enough amphetamine to keep me sharp enough to not kill anyone. When we were deployed together, I never worried about her getting killed. But nothing kept me sane at home like loving her. She avoided her comfort zone, never got bored or was boring. She was serious but not dull. She was a bulwark against my worst impulses, and my God, my God I loved her more than I thought I could love anything.

Her opinion meant everything to me. She'd never think I was weak, yet I was terrified she would.

Truth incoming.

I didn't want her to tell me it was nothing, even though I hoped it was.

I didn't want her to have some easy cure, but I didn't want to continue like this.

I didn't want to become a patient in my own marriage.

I wanted it to go away by itself. Prove it was a bad day and that I could handle it at the same time.

But it didn't. The second night with no relief from the feeling something was there, as Greyson breathed softly next to me, I lay awake in the silent dark, trying to isolate the problem. If I could build a wall around this feeling, hem it in, maybe I could identify it and throw it away. Pick the shrapnel out of my own guts to *plink plink* in the tray, shard by shard, observe them without the crust of shit and blood.

I must have been seconds from sleep. The shadows got deeper, outlines shifting with the passage of the moon in the window, taking on new, more threatening shapes.

Threatening, and yet... not.

My shrapnel had a shape, and it was compassion. A silent empathy and gentleness just this side of sweet. The Thing watching me, wanting me, the violent pressure on my mind I'd just gotten a shape around had a personality, and it was *kind*.

My body jolted with a cortisol flood, waking Greyson. She sat up on one arm. Her long straight hair covered her face in a veil. "Caden?"

"It's okay," I said. "Just a dream."

Why the fuck did I say that?

"Can you tell me—?"

"No."

Twisting to her side, she lay down facing me, hands tucked

under her pillow. She stayed silent for a few seconds. "You should write it down."

"Go to sleep." I stroked her hair away from her face.

When I'd met her, she kept her hair just long enough to keep in a ponytail, but short enough to care for easily. Now that we were civilians, she was letting it grow.

I loved her so much, I wanted to marry her every single day for the rest of my life.

Then a realization hit me like Reveille in the morning.

The Thing? The pressure? The entity that had its own personality that was all gentle kindness?

The Thing loved her too.

Maybe my mental weakness came from being tired, or hiding things from Greyson. Maybe I was jealous of a figment of my imagination. Maybe I wanted to show it who was in charge here.

For all those reasons, and some more complex instinct, I ran my hand down her back. She wore satin nightgowns, a civilian pleasure she reserved for herself and me. She sighed when my palm landed on her ass.

"Doctor?" One eye opened under the web of hair that covered her face. "Do you know what time it is?"

"It's time for you to get on your hands and knees."

"Excuse me?"

I got up on my knees and grabbed her hips on either side, lifting them over the mattress. She flopped onto her hands, half twisted.

I bent my body over hers, reaching around her waist and talking softly in her ear. "If 'excuse me' means no, then say no."

She swiped her hand around her head to get the hair off her face, looking back at me with an unfiltered gaze. "It doesn't mean no, but..."

I pushed my hard cock against her ass, and she didn't finish the sentence. "Then you're excused."

I grabbed her breast harder than I normally would. She was mine. I would not be undercut, and I would not compete. I pulled her nightgown up and yanked down her underwear. Our eyes met over her shoulder as I got my cock out.

"I can't lean on the wrist for long," she said.

"I'm aware." Running the head of my dick along her seam, I spread her wetness onto myself, then I lodged myself in her. She gasped.

Normally, I'd gently slide in, but not this time. Something more primal called, and I shoved another few inches inside.

Yeah.

Just like I thought.

The Thing was horrified.

"Let's get pressure off that wrist." I took her by the biceps and pulled her arms behind her, holding them together with one hand. "Better?"

"Yes." Her head dropped forward.

"This is going to be different," I said.

"No shit."

I hesitated. My desire to show the Thing my dominance couldn't be satisfied at her expense. I loosened my grip on her arms just a little.

"Don't..." She stopped, took a deep breath, and turned her head as much as she could. "Don't stop. I'll let you know." Her hips pushed into me.

Gently, I gathered her hair with my free hand and wrapped it around my fist, then I yanked her head back as I entered her with full force.

She screamed through her teeth. "God! Caden!"

Her cunt pulsed around me as I hesitated again.

"Say no," I growled.

"Yes."

I fucked her so rough, I didn't expect her to come so hard and so quickly. I kept fucking her, holding her arms behind her, pulling her hair as if it were a bridle. I unleashed deep inside her, bruising her arms with my grasp.

Right there, a whirlwind spun around us as I pounded her, whipping me into a confusion of desire and need, surrender and dominance. Even as I thrust forward physically, mentally I was spun by the force of it. Flipped like a coin, revolving in the air, landing, settling on the mattress.

The whirlwind fell away, and there was only Greyson under me.

The kind, sweet Thing shrank back into the shadows, weeping.

Take that, you fuck.

Chapter Six

GREYSON

In the weeks after he took me from behind in the middle of the night, we went back to normal. The episode seemed like a pleasurable blip in a pleasurable routine.

We were meeting at the Mt. Sinai fundraiser. It was a cutting day. When he arrived at the fundraiser, he'd smell of rubbing alcohol and cologne if he'd put some on, fresh coffee grounds and cut grass if he hadn't. He'd touch my shoulder. He'd run his finger along the edge of my strapless gown. At home, we'd barely make it in the door before he'd strip me naked and take me. Yes, it was predictable. Some things were worth predicting.

I crawled into the back of the car where my younger brother, Colin, waited. He was an engineer who'd been inspired to go to college after I'd found a way to go to med school, and he'd moved to New York for a job just as I was settling in. The education had done nothing to tamp his roguish ways.

"You look nice," he said when I slid in next to him. He flicked one of my dangling earrings.

"You do too." I straightened his black bow tie as the limo coasted toward the museum.

He shooed my hand away. "Thanks for the plus one."

"Try to keep off the ladies."

"What's the fun in that when I have to watch your husband with his hands all over you?"

"Stop it."

"You two are so in love it makes me sick."

I looked away, trying to hide my silent laughter. "What happened to you and that woman? The painter? She seemed nice."

"She wanted things."

"Things?"

"Promises. Commitments. Me. I have things I'm doing. I can't get sidetracked by a pretty face." He tapped his knee for a second. "Or all the other things. Whatever. How's the practice coming?"

"Not bad," I said. "Better."

"You like it?"

"I love it. We're here. Put your jacket on."

THE EVENT TOOK place in a ballroom lined with Regency-era portraits and heavy drapery. I plucked a champagne flute from a server's silver tray and Colin did the same.

"This is lovely." He scanned the room like a cheetah selecting the weakest in the herd.

"Behave."

"Oh, your friend Jenn is here. I like her," he purred.

I elbowed him as Jenn saw us and headed over. She was awkward in heels and her fat black glasses always slid down her nose, but her smile was a beacon of light against her brown skin. We greeted each other, and she swapped her empty flute for a full one.

"Easy there, tiger," Colin said.

Jenn took no shit, and she was a terrible flirt. "I'm grown, but thank you."

"He's on the make," I offered.

"Good luck with that." She tipped her glass to him, and he responded with a clink. "Ronin's here," she said to me.

"Where is he?" I craned my neck. "He sent me some referrals. I owe him a drink."

I saw him before the last word was out of my mouth, but he already had a drink in his hand. He wedged his way through the crowd toward us.

"What are you doing here?" I asked as he kissed my cheek.

"Business."

"Obviously," Jenn said. "No one's here for the food."

"Thank you for the referrals," I said. "I owe you a drink."

"Open bar doesn't count."

We were talking about something unimportant when Ronin put his arm around my shoulders and pulled me to him, but we were laughing.

"Blah blah," Colin complained. "Caden's here."

He crossed the room to my husband, whose eyes were on me. Caden wore a deep navy suit and a gold tie. His cufflinks sparkled, and his hair was combed off his face. The fact that he hadn't shaved contrasted the crispness of the suit against the animal body inside it.

We went quiet. He wasn't looking at me. He was looking at Ronin.

Ronin removed his arm from my shoulders.

Colin interrupted the gaze by shaking my husband's hand and making some sort of wisecrack he must have found hilarious.

Caden, not as much. He'd turned his attention back to me.

"Girl. He looks like he wants to eat you alive," Jenn said into her glass.

I turned to Ronin so I could blame him, but he was gone. Caden maneuvered to us.

"My dad never looked at my mom like that," Jenn continued.

Before I could offer a snappy answer, Caden found us and kissed Jenn on the cheek. He kissed my cheek in the same platonic way, then looked behind him, but no one was there.

"Where's Colin?" I asked.

"Bar."

When I turned to scan the bar for my brother, I leaned into Caden a little. We had a pattern. A rhythm to our interactions. The shape of the space between us, laid out over the time together, was as predictable as the phases of the moon, and his touch always came when expected.

But when we looked at Colin as he tried to charm a young lady in a gold dress, Caden didn't lean in when I did. He didn't put his hand on my back. When Bob Abramson found me and said he wanted me to meet someone, my husband didn't take my hand. When Wilhelmina, the head cardiac nurse, her hair braided into long, neat rows, gave me a kiss and asked how I was handling my husband's hours, Caden didn't come close to me and brush his thumb between my shoulder blades. When we all sat down for a presentation about the hospital's goals, he kept his hands folded in his lap.

When he released his hands and placed them on his knees, I put my left hand over his right. He patted it, smiled at me, and slipped it away before looking behind him again.

I thought he was in a bad mood.

What else could it be?

Chapter Seven

CADEN

The war had been building for over a month. The ventilators were left to do their job, but the squeak of gurney wheels on linoleum, the tip-tap of computer keys, the murmurs of the hospital staff all held a thread of the Thing I thought I'd banished. I could have a conversation with Greyson, but only if I concentrated on not hearing the Thing in the boiling pasta water or the radio news. Every day, it got a little stronger. Every day I was a little more tense, a little more afraid, a little more uncomfortable. The Thing got harder to box away and cart off. Harder to hide behind a wall. Impossible to ignore. I was pressed in on all sides by a Thing I couldn't even define.

And what had become more and more clear was that it wanted my wife.

"CADEN!"

I was in the changing room, getting my scrubs off, when Bob Abramson, the hospital director, came in. My senseless, gland-centric reaction was anger. He wanted her too, but for different reasons.

"Bob." I got my suit out of the locker.

"Are you going to the fundraiser tonight?"

"Yes. Why?"

"Tina Molino from the psych hospital's going. You should introduce yourself."

I slapped my locker door closed so hard it rattled. "I know her. She had a lot of questions about military trauma. I guess the Gibson wing's going through then?"

"Anything's possible with funding."

"I know you're eyeing my wife." That came out wrong. Wrestling with this Thing and trying to have a conversation with my boss was crossing my wires.

He overlooked my words in favor of my intentions. "She's got the right history. She understands the military. Has done a ton of PTSD work. We could really use her."

"Really?" I slid the padlock in the loop but didn't close it. I hadn't finished with the locker, but had slammed it closed to make a point. I didn't know what was wrong with me. I was jealous. Not sexually jealous. I was jealous of her time and attention. "Well, you can talk to her about it, but don't expect much. She's busy."

"The best ones are."

Getting snippy with the hospital director wasn't my best decision and it wasn't something I had control over, though of course, in the moment, it felt like the purest form of control. That was the thing about impulsive behavior. It hid behind a mask of power.

Greyson could handle herself. Everyone who wanted her for anything needed to be far away from me.

"Look," I said, "it's been a long day."

"No need to explain. You're barely out of your scrubs and I'm bugging you. It's fine. Say hello to Dr. Molino anyway."

"Yeah. Sure. Of course."

He left with a spring in his step. Nothing wiped the smile off that guy's face, but he was a shark. If he wanted Greyson for this psych unit, he'd have her. I knew it, and so did Abramson.

Opening my locker again, I got a whiff of her perfume. I couldn't resist taking it after I'd decided to starve the Thing out. Maybe that was why I'd failed to eradicate it.

I got dressed and walked out with Greyson on the brain. When the door *whoosh*ed closed, the sound was a sigh of longing for the only woman I'd ever loved. I locked it away.

I COULD PUT on a suit and knot a tie. I could put jeweled links into a starched cuff. I could shower, shave, comb my hair, but it was all a lie. It was all a costume, a mask. Under it, I was no more than a knot of bodily needs and overwhelming sexual urges. My mind was a set of neurons firing commands to my glands, and the glands sent emotions through my bloodstream.

She was mine.

Not his.

The Thing was male, and its strength was its persistence.

The neurons said I had to have her in my line of sight, but I'd bring the Thing right to her.

The only way to keep it away from her was to keep my distance.

But the animal said no. The animal I was knew that wouldn't work because she was mine.

Navigating between all these urges was exhausting. But as I entered the fundraiser, I took a breath. The exhaustion was under my suit. Behind my smile and polite words. No one could see.

She was with her brother and Jenn. Her hair was piled on top of her head and her earrings dropped down the length of her neck. She wore nude lipstick, and under the satin bodice of her gown, her nipples were hard. She was the picture of grace and charm, with a smile that transformed everyone around her and eyes that comforted people into talking.

The Thing saw her. In the bouncing acoustics of the room, it whispered its longing.

"Hello." Colin shook my hand.

I hadn't even seen him coming toward me. Just her. Only her.

"Nice to see you." I angled myself so I could see her over his shoulder.

"I'm hitting the bar, can I get you something?"

"I'm good, thanks." I patted his shoulder and headed for her, crossing half a ballroom without acknowledging another soul.

The Thing got more vocal, hiding in the voices of the guests and the strings of the musicians' instruments.

I could smell her from farther away than normal. Apples. No matter which perfume she wore, she smelled of the first bite of an apple, breaking taut skin with teeth, juice dripping down my chin. She was the satin skin and the crisp meat of the fruit. She was the hard seed and the tenacious stem.

I found her.

Ronin.

Laughing.

Arm around her shoulders.

He'd touched her. He'd had her. He'd licked the apples off her skin and touched her body. He wanted her again. Of course he did. She was beautiful and sexy. Any man would want her. I was filled with an unreasonable fury. A foul grimace in my soul. A call to action lubricated by rage.

I headed for them, bumping into a woman from pediatrics. I excused myself, and when I turned back, Ronin was gone.

In the seven steps to my wife, I came to some sort of sense.

Ronin was not a threat.

On the flip side, I was losing my fucking mind.

Kissing Jenn first was a delay tactic. I needed a moment to reduce my pulse rate. It didn't work. When I kissed Greyson's cheek and she slipped her hand in mine, the animal threatened to burst out of his suit.

I always desired her. Every minute. But this?

I wanted to drag her out by her hair, respecting the norms of privacy only because I wouldn't be able to finish in the middle of the ballroom. I wanted to squeeze her flesh, mark her in bruises, leave streaks of semen on her. Make the Thing scream in horror and curl up in a ball far away.

I couldn't live like this anymore.

But I was in a public place.

The suit was who I needed to be.

The suit was armor against the horrifying sight of the animal.

I didn't look at her. Didn't touch her. I focused on the distance between us and the eyes of a hundred people. I listened to Bob Abramson talk about money and bullshit, concentrating hard enough to make a decent show of being civilized.

In the dark, during the fundraising video, she leaned into me, taking my hand. "What's going on?"

"Nothing."

"Caden." My name was more than a statement. It was a comment on how well she knew the animal, and how well she loved it.

If eyes could listen, hers did, gazing at me in the darkness. I couldn't lie to her for much longer.

The entire invite list was watching the video. The bar was empty. The hallway lights were dimmed. The kitchen staff moved constantly and quietly to set up the buffet.

I laced my fingers in hers. She had a gold band we'd gotten out of expediency. No big sparkling rock. No sign I'd ever courted her properly before marrying her.

My father always said a man didn't skip steps if he wanted to do something once.

I slid my cheek to hers and whispered in her ear, "I want to destroy you."

Her hand tightened in mine so tightly I could feel our bones. Her glands must have fired, because the apples and the perfume melded and became something so uniquely *her* my balls ached—but not for simple release. For something more. An agreement of ownership.

Waiting wasn't an option.

Pulling her by the hand, I headed for the hallway.

"Caden," she said when we were away from the event, "slow down."

I didn't. I couldn't. I pulled her down the carpeted steps to the lower level, stepping over a velvet rope at the bottom. The lights were out in the hall. Three doors led to three empty event rooms.

"What's with you lately?" she asked.

"Are you saying no?"

"I'm asking a question."

I backed into one of the rooms and pulled her in. It was dark but for light coming from under the doorways on each side. The Thing cowered in the shadows, emitting fear like a pheromone. Good. I walked in deeper, eyes adjusting quickly enough to avoid the tables and stacks of chairs on wheeled dollies.

"So am I." I faced her. "Are you saying no?"

"What are you hoping I'll say yes to?"

"I'm going to pull that dress up until I can get to these hard nipples." I pinched them through the dress and she gasped. "Then I'll bend you over one of these tables and fuck you so hard walking's going to hurt. Are you saying no?"

"I'm not. But I want to know what's going on with you."

"Pull your dress up before I shred it."

Scaring her wasn't my plan, but there was fear in the air. I had no choice but to breathe it in.

The fear didn't come from her. As she pulled her dress over her waist to show me her thong and the lace edges of her stockings, she bit her lower lip. The fear I detected was in the shadows.

I stepped behind her.

The Thing was going to watch me.

I pushed my hand up between the fabric and her skin, taking that taunting nipple. I twisted it. Pulled. She gasped.

"Say stop if you need to." I drove my other hand under her thong and ran four fingers over her soaking cunt.

"Don't."

"Don't what?" I pushed my cock against her ass, speaking into her ear.

"Stop. Don't stop."

"Does it hurt?" I abused her nipple again.

"Yes."

"I should stop?"

"No."

I looked over her shoulder, into the shadows, and asked, "You like it?"

I pinched her clit, and she released an *nnn* sound through her teeth.

"Yes."

Yanking my hands away, I pushed her into a table, bending her sharply. When she tried to get up on her hands, I shoved her down by the base of her neck. Her earring fell over her jaw and clicked against the table.

Her ass was round and smooth in the dim light. Too perfect. Too well-formed. I slapped it. She gasped, trying to look back at me. I pushed her down harder and slapped again.

A little voice made me want to check on her again, but I slapped her one more time and she smiled.

That was all the answer I needed. I forgot about the Thing. Forgot about how much it wanted her. There was only Greyson and me in a dark room with our suddenly elastic boundaries. I ripped her thong at the crotch.

Unleashing my cock, I slapped her ass one more time before I set myself at her entrance. She braced, and I jammed into her. She grunted, because beneath the dress and the sparkling earrings, she was an animal too.

I took her, pressing her down at the jaw so I could hook my thumb in her mouth. "Who owns you?"

"Oh, God," she said around my thumb, eyelashes fluttering.

"Wrong answer." I thrust deep and hard. "Who owns your body?"

"You."

"Don't forget it. Do you hear me? You're mine. Your cunt is mine. Your tits are mine. You're going to come and that's mine."

We didn't talk like that, hadn't until that moment, and it was satisfying, as if I'd been waiting to say it for too long.

"Say it." I fucked her like a punishment, grinding deep. My thumb slid out of her mouth.

"My body is yours."

"That's right." I reached around and found her clit, flicking it. "Who owns this?"

"You."

"Say it." I rubbed it with all four fingers.

"My cunt is yours. Only you, Caden. Only you." She'd gone a step further than I asked, and my blood raced. Still, she went on. "I'm yours." She stifled a cry.

"You're going to come."

"Yes."

"It's mine."

"Yours."

She was so close. I leaned down and bit her trapezius as it tightened. Right at the base of her neck, clamping down until she jerked, and I growled in my throat, holding her still.

The whirlwind gathered and the Thing wept.

When I let go, she had a wet arc of marks where I could see

them. Perfect. Driving deep into her, I took her clit until her legs went stiff and her mouth opened in a silent scream.

Yes. That was mine. Her mindless pleasure. Her hooked fingers. Her red ass. My bite mark. The cyclone of desires surrounding us flipped me over again. I was her lover and her tormenter. Her husband and attacker. Her pain and my pleasure spinning in a centrifuge.

"I'm coming inside you," I spit out. She had to know or I'd keep spinning. "Because you're mine."

Filling her, I claimed her inside and out, and the whirlwind stopped.

Chapter Eight

GREYSON

I ached when I woke. From the bottom up: My feet from the shoes. My pussy from the sex. My trapezius muscle from the bite.

I bent over the bathroom vanity and ran my fingers over the bite bruise. It wasn't too bad. The skin was a shade redder. It looked like a mild hickey. My eyes were ringed in black. I hadn't bothered to take off my makeup. We'd had sex twice again at home, if you could call it sex. More like he took my body and made it his own, giving orgasms and taking them as if they were a marital right. I'd collapsed into unconsciousness.

I wiped the bluish-gray mascara stains from my face.

My body wasn't a marital right, of course. My body was my own, and I could refuse him at any time. Caden knew that. He must have, because even after we got home, he checked on me.

Twice, the mask of determination snapped off, leaving a man who looked disconcerted.

Twice, he asked me if I wanted to slow down or stop.

Once, I said I was fine. Once, I begged him not to stop.

Both times, his brutality returned like a Halloween mask on an elastic string.

I should have made him stop, but I couldn't.

Why?

Was I threatened? Did I believe he'd hurt me worse if I did? Would he?

No.

"No," I said into the mirror. "He wouldn't."

How did I know? Was it the orgasms he gave me? He'd acted as if my pleasure gave him power. Every orgasm drove him to greater intensity, and each increase in passion drove me deeper into a sexual fugue.

I trusted him. One, he was a doctor, and a great one. It didn't get any safer than that. Two, he wanted me to want what he did. The checking in told me that much. He wanted consent. Needed it as much as I did, but I didn't think... no, I was sure he hadn't planned the last two rough encounters, so he couldn't have asked ahead of time. He was getting the idea to hurt me in the moment.

The pain.

Next time, I should stop him when it hurt. When he bit me. When it was uncomfortable.

I should, but I wouldn't. Morning Greyson, with her mascara running down her face and a bite mark on her neck, knew it wasn't okay to cause your partner pain or discomfort during sex. Dr. Greyson Frazier knew it was okay as long as it was coupled with consent and clear boundaries.

She knew it had a name.

I tossed the mascara-streaked wipe into the trash and went downstairs before I could say the name to myself.

CADEN WAS AT THE STOVE, making breakfast. My favorite.

"Pancakes!" I fist pumped quietly. "Pow."

I kissed him and he looked down at me, mask gone. Just my husband. He moved the spatula to the other hand and squeezed my shoulders while he flipped the cakes.

"I have nothing today," he said. "What about you?"

"Session in the morning and that's it. I was going to go work out. Maybe. I don't know. It's still kind of weird, all this time to myself."

He laced his fingers in mine, nudging the disks around pensively. "You said a big rock didn't go with army green. What you wore last night would have been stunning with a ring."

Pulling his arm off my shoulder I put my left hand next to his. "We match. That works for me."

He shut off the stove and jerked the pan until the cakes slid. "Do you miss the service?"

He deserved my honesty, but there was more to the question than a simple lament for a job I didn't have anymore. He was the reason I'd left five weeks before instead of forty years from now.

But I couldn't lie to him or myself. "Sometimes."

He shifted the pan back and forth on the burner so the pancakes would skate around. "There's a thing at Chelsea Piers. Like a festival normal cities have with booths, et cetera."

"Normal cities?"

"Like where you grew up." He tipped the pan to slide the pancakes onto a plate. If I'd tried that, their skin would have stuck to the surface and been an entire disaster. Everything he did was so easy for him, as if the laws of physics were his to command.

"I grew up in six different cities."

"In any of them, did you have festivals and block parties and normal events where people spend money on garbage?"

"A couple."

"How normal."

He picked up the plate and looked right at me for the first time that morning. His gaze landed on the bite mark. Reflexively, I covered it. He put the plate down and moved my hand away.

"Broken blood vessels," he said. "You have some abrading to the skin."

"It's fine."

"Does it hurt?"

"Only when you touch it, so don't." I picked up the plate. "I'm starving."

I kissed him and went to the table. He'd set it with silverware and glasses, and as I draped the cloth napkin on my lap, I took a second to acknowledge that he didn't usually set up an elaborate breakfast. He cooked for me as often as I cooked for him, but this was a step beyond.

As if he was trying to get back into my good graces.

For the pain. For the roughness. For the use of my body.

There's a name for this.

WE TOOK a cab to the totally normal thing that normal cities have. Chelsea Piers members had priority entry before four o'clock, so we got in before it got too crowded.

I'd done some classes at the Piers. The sports facility was literally built on three piers that had fallen into disuse when New York was bankrupt. Now it was gorgeous. The warehouse-style buildings had an ice skating rink, a place for all kinds of sports, public spaces, and a driving range, which I'd never bothered with until that day.

We got to the water side of the facility and exited into the bright afternoon sun. The fairway usually had nets on either side to catch golf balls, but they'd been lowered. A Ferris wheel rotated against the blue sky, a band played light rock, and the smell of buttery popcorn filled the air. Yellow-and-blue-striped tents lined each side of the fairway, with hawkers promising more prizes than they would ever deliver.

I heard gunshots and the *whee* of mortar fire.

My bloodstream flooded with the desire to run, pushing every coherent thought right out of my head. I ducked in time for the explosion, which came canned for civilian ears.

Caden pulled me up and held still as if he wanted to shield me with his body.

The *whee* resumed, but without the surprise, it sounded as canned as the explosion, coming from a single point on the left instead of moving through space. Caden's hold on me relaxed.

The explosion came with another *whee*. I followed his gaze to a pellet gun game. The mortar fire was just for effect, so the players could feel as if they were on the front lines.

"It's a game." He brushed hair off my face. "Let's get away from it."

He tried to guide me to the other side of the fairway, but I wouldn't budge. "No. They need to tell people."

I walked right up to the booth with my fists in a bunch. The squealing of little bombs and snapping of pellets sent shockwaves through a brain stem already firing on all cylinders.

When I got there, a white kid of about sixteen, with red bumps all over his cheeks, was making change out of the leather apron.

I wasn't going to yell at him. It wasn't his fault I was afraid. It wasn't mine either, but that wasn't the point. I hated it. I hated being at the mercy of a noise. I hated that I couldn't do something because of my own limitations. That was crap. I didn't believe in limitations. I didn't believe in self-imposed redlines.

I was going to break this shit into a million pieces, right there, right then.

I dug into my pocket and found a few dollars. I was about to slap them on the counter when Caden pushed my hand down and laid two twenties on the wood, tapping it.

"You sure?" he asked.

He knew what I was doing. He didn't have to ask and I didn't need to explain. He knew I needed to smash a boundary.

"Are you?"

"You're the one with the scar." His gaze toward my chest wasn't sexual. The wound I'd sustained when a mortar arced over the wire had left a scar under my shirt and, unexpectedly, in my mind.

"I'm just jumpy. It's not a big deal."

"Welcome," the kid said. "Shoot out the star and win a prize."

"She's going to shoot until she says she's done."

"Yes, sir." He took a twenty and made change. "Prize is for the entire star. No red—"

"Yeah," I interrupted, lifting the rifle in front of me. "We got it."

Whee.

In the first burst, I missed the target entirely because my adrenal glands were pumping pure fire through my veins. I wiped my palm on my jeans.

"You all right?" Caden asked.

I put my eye in the sight. "Yeah."

"You can't win once you miss. You need every pellet," the kid said.

"I'm not here to win a giant stuffed dog."

As long as my finger was on the trigger, the sound of whistling and exploding bombs continued. I squeezed off the rest of the pellets. *Pop-pop-pop,* then the click of an empty magazine ended the bombs. I shook out my wrist. Caden called over the kid in the leather vest, and he reloaded. I was sweating, tingling, jumping out of my skin. I didn't have a drop of spit in my mouth.

"You're white as a sheet," Caden said with true concern. "All the blood's rushed to your extremities."

"Yeah."

I picked up the rifle and did it again. This time, Caden had the kid set up the rifle next to me so I didn't have to wait for a reload. I shot at stars until my hand hurt and the sound of mortar fire was background noise. My husband took out more money, and I pumped a bunch of lead at nothing until my body couldn't maintain the adrenaline dump anymore and the pain in my wrist had gone from a dull ache to a numb tingle.

I held up my hands. "I'm done."

Caden took my wrist and checked my pulse. "Ninety-two." He held me, kissing my temple. I was shaking. "You're amazing."

"I am!"

"Ah, the endorphins." He was laughing, and I laughed with him.

"Hey! Lady!" the kid in the leather vest called. "You can pick one of these." He pointed at a low shelf of prizes. "A snake or a dog."

I leaned over the counter. I wasn't interested in either the green foot-long stuffed snake or the furry brown dog.

"My girlfriend has a snake. It fits under her neck when she sleeps."

"Sold!"

He tossed me the prize. "Don't join the army. You're a lousy shot."

"Thanks for the advice!"

Caden put his arm around me, snickering at the kid's comment. "What else do you want to conquer today?"

"The world!"

Skipping on air, we got popcorn and beer. I forgot to worry about the bite on my neck or how much I'd liked getting it. I let go of the word that brought to mind and all the psychology behind it. I rejected things in myself I was trained to accept in other people, so I didn't think of the word in relation to myself. I didn't think about anything but Caden and how happy he looked when he fed me popcorn.

A cheer went up from a crowd, and we turned to it.

A tower crane rose from a fixed base in the water. Cranes were normal in New York, apparently. It seemed as if something was always being built, and of course everything was tall.

But this crane had a person dangling from the end of it. Their arms and legs were splayed like a starfish as the line behind them got longer to lower them to the ground.

"You want to bungee jump?" Caden asked. "Get fear of heights off the table?"

"Could you watch me fall?"

Caden's parents had died in 9/11. When nothing was found of them but his mother's shoe, he'd convinced himself they'd jumped over a hundred stories.

"Negative." He dropped the popcorn container in the trash and held out his hand. "Let's go."

I took his hand and pulled him toward the jump. "Watching me fall is a great way of overcoming your own fear."

He yanked me toward him. "You'd do that for me?"

I looked up at the crane as someone fell, and I shuddered. My first fall was at six years old, from the top of the monkey bars. I'd cut open my lip and broken a clavicle, but what I remembered was how powerless I felt on the way down; how long it took and how many seconds I spent waiting for impact. Then while in the ROTC program at UCLA, I was making out with Scott Verehoven on the high dive, where—being a diver no girl said no to—he was perfectly comfortable. However, I said no because in the first place, I didn't think he was worth it and in the second, I didn't think it was safe. Nor did I trust him to keep me from falling. He proved all three points by pushing me over.

The fact that I could swim didn't make it funny in the least. If I was half afraid of heights from breaking my collarbone on the monkey bars, I was fully terrified once Scott pulled me out of the pool with a sprained neck and half my body richly bruised from my collision with the water.

I wasn't bungee jumping off a crane. No way. My endorphins had been reabsorbed. I wasn't all-powerful anymore.

"Nope." My hands slashed the air. "Changed my mind."

"All right. No heights today. Hey," he interrupted himself as if that was the only way he was going to say what he needed to. "Last night."

"Yes?"

"It's not going to happen again."

"Oh?" I almost said, "why not?" as if I wanted to get bitten again, which I did. But I didn't want to tell him that, because there was a name for someone who got sexual pleasure from pain and I wasn't ready to say it out loud.

"Yeah. And I'm sorry."

"If you were doing something to be sorry for, I would have said stop."

"In any case. That wasn't okay." He took me by the chin and kissed me. "Thank you."

He wasn't getting it. Maybe I wasn't either.

WE MADE LOVE THAT AFTERNOON.

And by "made love," I mean we fucked passionately and considerately. We used our mouths for pleasure. He eased into me with grace, touched me where I liked to be touched, made sure I came long and hard before he did.

The bite mark was gone the next day, and though I didn't forget about the self-doubt it had revealed, I didn't think about it much because I didn't want to.

Two weeks passed.

I picked up two more clients from Ronin, which pretty much filled my schedule. I seemed to have a gift for counseling and medicating PTSD. Go figure. My military life was of use, and as that became apparent, I missed it less and less.

One night, as I was coming out of the bathroom, I caught Caden looking into an empty corner. I say "caught" because when he heard me, he jumped as if he was doing something wrong, then he passed me to go into the bathroom without saying a word or touching me.

He usually found some way to touch me.

The last lack of affection had ended at the fundraiser where he'd fucked me on a banquet hall table. Brutal sex after days of growing emotional distance. And boom, fixed the next morning as if nothing had happened.

Was he having an affair?

I felt every pulse of blood through my veins, hot with sparking electricity at the thought of his body touching another woman's.

I breathed through it, telling myself nice things about trust and the basic goodness inside my husband. It worked to clear the room of the noise, but the hum of possibility remained in the corners, cowed but not killed.

I DIDN'T HAVE time to see Jenn's show. Not really. I had an emergency session with a new patient who hadn't slept in a week. His wife had called me in desperation. He was having aural hallucinations and she couldn't tell if it was the exhaustion or the PTSD.

I met him, wrote him a script, and didn't have a place in my schedule to see him until he started crying. A grown man. A soldier. Six feet tall and two hundred pounds of muscle, weeping in my office.

And I got upset when my husband was a little distant.

I handed the patient a tissue. He cracked his neck and got on with it. Maybe I needed to relax on Caden a little.

Deciding I didn't need lunch on Wednesdays, I fit him into my schedule. Then I got a cab to 57th Street while it was still daylight.

"Here!" The driver pulled over in front of the Kadousian Gallery.

From the street, I saw Jenn, in baggy overalls and Vans, animatedly talking to people I couldn't discern past the glass's reflection. Rows of painted masks hung on the walls.

Jenn saw me and opened the glass door. "Hey!"

We hugged, and she introduced me to her guests. Tina Molino of Mt. Sinai's Psychiatric Division, and Dylan Coda from the VA Hospital in Newark.

"I'm sorry I'm late. I had an emergency."

"I was just telling Tina she works in the same hospital as your husband."

Tina was almost six feet tall with a black bob, white skin, and red lipstick. She looked like Snow White. "I was hoping to meet you at the fundraiser. Caden St. John is quite a star around the doctors' lounge."

"Careful. His ego can get to the size of a blimp."

"You trained him well."

"War makes men humble."

"Nice segue." Jenn held her hand out to the rows of masks and began the tour. "All of these were made by vets as part of the NEA's Creative Forces program."

I WAS HALFWAY DOWN the block when I heard a woman's voice calling my name.

Tina scurried toward me. "Hey, I wanted to talk to you. Do you have a minute?"

I looked at my watch. "I have about eleven if there's no traffic uptown."

"It's enough."

We went into the little coffee shop wedged between a FedEx and an office building. We had our coffee in ninety seconds and seats on the window ledge in five more.

"Okay. Jenn told me you're an officer and an MD specializing in PTSD in vets."

"Kind of fell into it. But yeah."

"Do you like it? I'm trying to hurry so I don't keep you."

"Do I have to answer quickly?"

"Take your time." She sipped her coffee, leaving red lipmarks on the plastic top.

"I'm from a military family. I enlisted at eighteen."

"Wow."

"Yeah. It was the only life I knew. Then I met Caden, and he wanted to go into private practice. So I left the army and came here with him. I thought I'd never feel right as a civilian, and New York... my God, there's no place in the world more overwhelming."

"That's the truth."

We tapped our coffee cups together.

"Helping these men and women... they're broken, but working with them makes me feel like I'm home. I love it."

"That's..." She shook her head in appreciation. "I'm glad to hear that. We're tackling a mental health unit to serve the military and—here's the newish thing—civilian contractors. Anyone who's worked in war. We're financed by Darren Gibson, and I think I may have an opportunity for you."

Chapter Nine

CADEN

Greyson spit toothpaste into the sink. When she ran the faucet, the Thing spoke inside the gurgling water. When she took the water in her mouth and her lips tightened and moved when she swished, my inner cold ran boiling hot.

She spit the water, and the Thing dispersed into the air vents, the fogged mirror, the space between my feet and the floor. It snaked around my wife's voice when she spoke. "She wants to talk to me about creating a treatment protocol for PTSD in vets. Then she's thinking of maybe expanding it to the general population. Kids and adults dealing with trauma."

She shook excess water off the brush and popped it into the cup. I didn't know how much longer I could last.

She was wearing a big T-shirt and underpants. Her feet were bare. Her nipples were hard. She was talking about Tina's offer to design programs at the Gibson Center, which wasn't really an offer but more of a suggestion to talk more. She was overwhelmed. She hadn't been in professional life very long.

"When I was promoted before, it was all forms and steps," she said. "Now it's fuzzier, you know?"

Sure. I knew.

"I thought you had a full schedule."

"I'm thinking I can squeeze it in."

There were reasons she shouldn't. She'd push herself to exhaustion. No one was here to give her limits. There was no ceiling or walls on what she could accept. This wasn't the army.

She crawled onto the bed and flopped into a sitting position with her back against the headboard.

The reasons she shouldn't do too much were easily explainable, but if I explained them, she'd fight me. I didn't want to fight. I didn't want to get angry, or I'd lose it again and hurt her. I didn't want to feel anything. I wanted this deadness, needed it to dampen the fear and anger.

"What do you think?" she asked.

"Did she tell you the salary?"

"No, I mean about..." She spread her legs.

I'd made love to her two nights ago and had barely kept myself from hurting her. I'd had to keep my hands on the bed and let her ride me. The Thing had been watching. If I touched her now, I would tear her apart to get rid of it.

I ran my hand inside her thigh and stopped.

The sense I wasn't alone was worse when I touched her.

"What?" She pouted.

"Touch yourself."

She bit her lower lip and slid her fingers under the crotch of her underwear.

Was It watching her? Hard to tell, but the feeling wasn't as strong.

She groaned. I was aroused, but I didn't have an emotional response to this beautiful woman running her fingers along her seam.

"I'm so wet for you," she said.

"Don't stop." Was my voice as emotionless and robotic to her as it was to me?

"I want you to fuck me."

"Faster." I stood over her and undid my pants. She reached for me, but I swatted her away.

"Tease," she said when I released my dick and fisted it.

"Pick up your shirt."

She showed me her tits. I felt the Thing stretching at the edge of my perception, trying to get in on the action, but for some reason, without a connection between Greyson and me, the circuit wasn't closed. It could feel what was happening, but not see it, or the other way around.

Fuck you, Thing. This one's for you.

I grunted. "Let me see you come."

In another minute, she was pumping her hips under her fingers with heavy, wet breaths. I came over her, leaving my semen streaked over her body.

She moaned with a satisfied *mmm* and took her hand from between her legs. I snapped tissues out of the box and wiped her up with all the tenderness of a clinician.

"Thank you." She smiled. "Come to bed."

I couldn't. I knew I couldn't but couldn't avoid it.

I loved her, but I felt nothing. My balls were empty and my heart was dead.

My beeper went off.

"Shit," she said. "Ignore it."

I picked it up, thanking God without the actual feeling of gratitude. "Hospital."

She sighed.

"Greyson." I was this close to telling her everything. If I didn't have an emergency to attend to, I would have, right then. Instead, I said, "I'm sorry."

"This is the life of a surgeon's wife."

I kissed her forehead and left without looking back.

This wasn't sustainable.

I MANAGED to stay at the hospital through the next day. I didn't know what I hoped for except this Thing would go away if I starved it of my wife's presence.

The surgery wasn't done until early morning. I showered in the attending lounge and collapsed on one of the cots. The Thing missed her. Its longing whispered through the air conditioning. I could spite it indefinitely, but I didn't know how long I could spite myself. I missed her already. We'd spent plenty of time apart, but I'd gotten spoiled. If she was next to me, she was safe. Knowing that helped me rest.

I was awake when she beeped me. I called her back, still on my back on a narrow cot.

"Hello," I said. "What are you doing up? It's not even six."

"I woke up and couldn't get back to sleep." Her voice was husky and broken.

At the sound of her voice, it softened like a puppy and vibrated off the walls. It was worried about her.

"Figured I'd start working on Tina's proposal," she said.

"Don't burn yourself out."

"I won't. Are you coming home?"

"I have to check the post-op report in a few hours."

"Okay. I know you're tired."

"I am."

"We have tickets to a play tonight."

Shit. How long would it take to starve this Thing? The room was dark, but I covered my eyes with my wrist to block it out. "What time?"

"Seating's at eight."

I could fake a surgery. I could fake being tired. I could take a trip. Starve it out. I didn't know if that was even an option, but it was the only idea I had.

Tell her you have to be in the OR.

No words came. I couldn't lie. I could make the words in my head but couldn't get them out.

It wasn't that I couldn't speak. I couldn't *lie*. And I knew, as sure as I knew the boundaries of the dark room I'd gotten up to pace across, that I couldn't lie because my emotions were stuffed in a bag and sealed away. Lying meant I had to fear the truth, which I didn't, and it meant I had to create fake vocal nuance, which I couldn't.

Hiding my emotions had been intentional, but easier than ever. The process of detachment had become greased. Frictionless. I barely had to think about it. I wasn't nervous. Wasn't panicky. I was curious about my feelings, what they'd been and how they drove me to lie. Why would a person lie unless there was a reward for it?

"Okay. I'll meet you there."

"Barring unforseens."

"Yes," I said. "Barring unforseens."

"I love you, Caden."

"I love you too."

I hung up, and with the separation, the Thing became clear in my mind. Very loud. And for the first time, it had a well-defined thought I could read.

You don't love her. I do.

THE FRONT DESK had a vertical whiteboard with the rooms, procedures, and the doctors performing. I scanned it as Wilhelmina picked up the eraser.

"Looking for something, doctor?" she asked, getting up on a stool to reach the top.

"Not yet."

Checking her clipboard, she erased Dr. Everett's name.

"What happened to Everett?" I asked.

"Strep."

Nurse Bergstrom picked up the phone. "Samuelson's on call."

"I have it," I cut in.

Wil looked at me as if I'd just clucked like a chicken. "It's an assist."

"I know. It's fine. I got it."

Will shrugged and wrote *St. John* in the empty space.

Chapter Ten

GREYSON

Caden wasn't going to make it to the play. My answering service picked up the message, and delivered it as I was putting on my shoes. He'd taken on another patient, and the patient needed pre-op monitoring.

I should have gone myself, but I didn't want to. I wanted to go with him.

He'd been worried I was going to burn out, but maybe he was the one who needed to snuff one end of the candle. And maybe this was why he'd been so distant and preoccupied.

Maybe.

People weren't always predictable. They didn't react the same exact way even when in very similar situations.

The last time I'd seen Caden under tremendous stress was during the war, and he hadn't been rigid and distant. On the contrary, even when he was closest to his breaking point, he'd been funny, even charming, as day three of his hands in men's bodies crested into day four without relief. I was giving him vitamin shots and an uncomfortable amount of amphetamine. He seemed to thrive, and yet... no one thrives when someone loses an arm or a leg on the table and you have to move to the next without a break.

He was like a carnival wheel spinning long after the barker's hand had left the rail. Spiraling on his own juice and energy, ball bearings lubricated to go on and on, he couldn't calm himself. Even after I'd given him a sedative, he couldn't sleep. I'd crawled onto the mattress with him, and finally, relieved of a single thing to do but sleep, he held me in his bed.

I knew how to be detached. My job required it. But I couldn't be. Not with him. At first, he hadn't been more to me than the next overworked army doc. But he was the only one I'd ever let pull me onto his cot fully clothed. He wasn't the only one who had wept with me, but he was the only one I'd wept with.

Was this what it was to love someone? To have that wall of detachment crumble and be rebuilt into a bridge?

I thought so. I swore it to myself because after those hours, we were so real together no one had to ask what was going on. Caden and I were an incurable condition.

Dispassion had a place in our lives, but not with each other.

The situation was different now. We were civilians living in New York City, not soldiers trying to save people in a war zone. Maybe I shouldn't be surprised or concerned by his distance.

He might be far away for a reason that had nothing to do with me or our marriage. Maybe it was him, just him.

"Is everything all right?" he asked after I'd beeped him twice. His voice was flat, as if he was asking a patient if they were in any pain and could they please describe it.

"You're not home," I said, meaning something completely different.

There's a nagging ache in the center of my chest.

"I had rounds." He had a different meaning under his answer.

On a scale of one to ten, with ten being unbearable, how would you rate your pain?

"I missed you at dinner," I said.

I want to say it's a three, but it's closer to a seven.

"I missed you too."

Here's an aspirin.

"When are you coming home?"

Maybe I can have something stronger?

"Samuelson's got strep. I have to fill in for him again."

No.

"Okay."

I'll manage then.

"I love you."

Maybe try acupuncture.

"Yeah." I hung up the phone.

Shove it.

MID-AFTERNOON.

I'd been in session all morning. I heard Caden upstairs while I was with a patient, heard the old pipes rattle in the walls when the shower went on, then saw his feet come down the front steps. I was seeing a patient in and couldn't catch Caden without disrupting the gentle flow that was part of my job.

"How were you this week?" I asked Specialist Leslie Yarrow, who liked to sit in the chair with the high cushions. She still wore her dog tags under her polo T-shirt and kept her hair very short. She'd been sent home with a shoulder injury that was healing better than her mind.

"Fine. Good." She shifted in her seat. She'd had a hard time sitting still since she got back.

"Did you sleep?"

"Some. The pills helped. Thank you."

"But not entirely?"

"Nah." She flipped it off as if it wasn't a big deal, but her eyes were ringed in pink and purple.

"Did you have the dream again?"

"Yeah."

The dream was a recounting of a child torn apart by an IED. She'd been eight and screaming in pain. When Leslie recalled the memory, she said she screamed for hours while she tried to find a medic, but on further investigation, it had been a minute and a half before the girl died in her arms.

In the dream, the girl was her daughter.

"Something this week... my wife got freaked out. She said I should tell you."

"Should you?"

"Yeah, probably."

I waited.

"When I woke up from it, I didn't know Mindy."

"How so?"

"I went into her room, and I knew the room and all the stuff. But the kid sleeping there? I was like, who is she? She was a stranger."

"How long did that last?"

"A minute... maybe ten. Molly came into the kitchen and was like, 'Are you going to wake her up for school or what?' and then I came to."

"So you'd describe it as a fugue state? Did you have the feeling you were half asleep?"

"I was... I forgot the entire thing after not knowing Mindy." She shrugged, and that wasn't a normal reaction for someone who'd lost a bunch of time.

"Is that the first time it happened?"

She looked away. "Yeah. I told Molly I really didn't want to talk about this."

I wasn't letting her off the hook. We had four minutes, and it was hers to use to talk or not. Her decision, not mine.

"When I was a kid, I lost some stuff. Few hours here and there." She shifted in her seat. "My dad used to come to my room and do things. It was... I knew he did it, but I would forget the actual *thing* if you know what I mean." She made a nervous laugh, and I held onto a non-judgmental, non-enraged, almost inhuman detachment.

"I want to pause for a second. I heard both parts of that, and if you—"

"Is it time to go yet?"

"We have a couple of minutes"

"I don't want to talk about this right now, okay?"

"Okay, but you're safe here. Any time."

She stood. "I should get going."

I adjusted her sleeping pill dosage and asked her to keep a log of any more feelings that she wasn't where she was supposed to be, or that she didn't know the people around her. She agreed, apologized profusely, and left.

I hurt for the little girl she had been, and promised myself I'd do everything I could to help the woman who came to my office.

I briefly made the connection between Leslie Yarrow's dissociation and my husband's. It was a symptom of PTSD and needn't be a personal betrayal.

That realization was my medicine for the rest of the day.

IT WAS dark by the time I went back up to the house. Everything was perfect. He hadn't left a crumb behind. Not a note or a rumpled sheet.

Calling got me his voice mail. I beeped him, but he didn't call back right away. I heated up dinner. Got into my pajamas. Put on the TV. Shut it off. Listened to the traffic outside. Went to the bathroom.

His clothes were in the hamper. Underwear. Slacks. A pale blue shirt that brought out the depth of his eyes. I gathered it in my hands and pressed it to my face, expecting to smell fresh coffee grounds in stale sweat.

I got something much more floral.

Feminine.

This is not cologne.

My blood took a second to boil. In that pause, I checked again. Definitely perfume.

Oh, fuck no.

No no no.

I was out the door so fast I didn't change out of my pajamas and almost forgot to put on shoes. I stuffed my feet into Keds, put on a long coat, and caught a cab at Columbus Circle.

Because, no. We had a deal and the deal included fidelity. Non-negotiable.

Deep breath.

People cheated for a reason. Either it was personal, and they were just cheating assholes. Or it was situational, and a cheating asshole was in a situation where it was easy to cheat. Or it was us. And that last option stuck in my craw, because even after years of talking to people about why they found themselves betraying or betrayed, it was now me. And if it was the relationship, it was me, my fault, what I delivered or didn't deliver.

I'd come to a strange life in a strange city to be with him. Maybe that was the problem. Or maybe we didn't work as a couple outside a war zone. Or maybe he liked it hotter than I was used to.

Fuck this. It wasn't my fault.

He owed me better than touching another woman. Saying

sweet things to her. Those were my kisses and sweet words.

Or maybe there was none of that. Maybe it was all warm holes and quick spurts.

The disloyalty was bad, but not knowing the exact terms of the betrayal was eating every brain cell not occupied with breathing.

My phone rang on the way. I flipped it open.

Him.

Was his dick wet with her? Or was he on his way there?

"Hi," I said.

"Hey, you called?" Flat flat flat. Why hadn't I seen it before? How blind had I been?

"Where are you? I was thinking of bringing you dinner."

"Ah, that would be great, but I'm assisting in an hour and I need to scrub in."

So that's what you sound like when you lie?

"Oh, all right then. When do you think you'll be home?"

"I came home today and you were in your office. I didn't want to bother you."

You knew I'd be in session.

"Yeah. Hey, the other line's beeping. I have to go."

"I love you," he said before I cut the call.

"Thanks for the aspirin."

WILHELMINA WAS at the front desk of cardiac. She confirmed Caden was scrubbing into an emergency open heart procedure. I told her I needed a key and he had it in his bag. I didn't like lying, but I was past sense. I was cussing up a blue streak in my head and smiling on the outside as if showing up at the hospital in Keds and a long coat was the result of an annoying misplaced key.

She led me into a row of large grey lockers and left me alone.

I tipped his padlock up to see the numbered dials. It was the same lock he'd had in Iraq, and I knew the combination.

Every marriage has boundaries, and going into his locker had a thick red line around it. My thumbnail in the grooves, I clicked the number sequence, paused with the weight in my hand.

Just ask him.

The mature thing to do would be to ask. Just say flat out, you've been different. You've been unavailable. You've got perfume on your shirt.

Fuck that.

I snapped the padlock open and slid it out quickly, before I could change my mind.

The locker was the size of a small closet. He had a suit, shoes on the floor, bag of toiletries on the top shelf, new clothes still in tissue paper in a Barney's bag, and a plastic bag of dirty things.

I picked up the dirties. I smelled it before I even opened the bag. Perfume.

"Fuck you, Caden."

I threw the bag back in and slammed the door. Something clicked and fell.

If one thing is out of order...

"I don't care."

...he'll know.

"I don't." I put the lock in the loop.

You'll never know if he would have told you the truth.

"Fuck!"

I opened the locker and readjusted the laundry bag. I couldn't find what had fallen. I tiptoed so I could see the top shelf. Next to the toiletry bag, a glass bottle lay on its side. I picked it up. It was from Lyric scent shop, where I got my perfume.

Before I even turned it over, I knew.

Scent #6512 - Greyson F.

Before I opened the top and waved it in front of my nose, I knew.

It was mine. I hadn't recognized it mixed with his scent, but once I had the bottle under my nose, it was unmistakable.

When we were separated, he'd given me one of his T-shirts. His smell had comforted me. I buried my face in it when he called, wrapped it around my neck when I slept, curled around it when I brought myself to orgasm.

When had he taken my perfume? And why? Did he know he'd be gone for days?

I put the bottle back and put the padlock back in place, touching the door with my fingertips. "I'm sorry."

Across the room, the door opened. I peeked around the lockers to find a cleaning person wheeling in a yellow bucket.

"Hello?" he called. "Anyone in here?"

"Just leaving," I said, smiling stiffly as I walked by.

"DID YOU FIND THE KEY?" Wilhelmina asked blithely, as if nothing was wrong. She could see into my heart and all was well there.

"I realized I had it."

"Ah, better watch, doctor. When the mind starts going, the body's sure to follow."

I laughed a little, but it was more from uneasiness than humor. "Do you know where he is?"

She slid a clipboard into a cubby. "I think he's in five." She took a quick inventory of my posture, my hair, my coat and pajamas, the look of emotional desperation that must have been all over my face, using a skill they didn't teach in nursing school but a large number of nurses had. "It's a viewing theater, if you want to take a look."

"Um, sure. Okay. Yeah. Yes, I'd like that very much."

I didn't know what insight I expected to get from watching him. Something was still off. My perfume didn't change that. But Wil led me to the upper floor viewing room where med students watched the procedure. I sat away from them, letting the narration from their instructor fade into the ambient hiss of the air conditioning.

From above, I saw him and the other attending move together with an efficiency bordering on grace. They cut a woman open and spread her ribs. I flinched. It was hard to watch.

But still, my husband did his job, isolating a living, beating heart.

The lead turned away from the table and looked up at the med students. Her voice carried over speakers to the little room as she spoke a language I hadn't been trained in med school to understand. My eyes were glued to my husband anyway. He was still working, though I couldn't discern what he was doing. When the lead surgeon said his name, it cut through the jargon.

"Doctor St. John here is assisting, but he's been lead on this procedure a few hundred times."

Caden looked up to salute the students.

He saw me and froze.

We didn't move as the other doctor continued. His eyes betrayed nothing. I was wrong to be here. Wrong to distrust him. Wrong to worry. He had his hands on a living heart. Of course his detachment bled over.

I waved and tried to smile.

He nodded and got back to work.

HE CALLED after one in the morning. I was in bed, watching the clouds cross the setting moon over the brownstones across the street.

"Did I wake you?" he asked. The vocal deadness was still there. Maybe I'd have to get used to it.

"No."

"Did you enjoy the surgery?"

"Better than *Cats*."

He laughed a real, true, guttural laugh and I almost burst into tears.

"I'm sorry," I said. "I disturbed you."

"You didn't disturb me."

"I missed you."

He sighed. It wasn't an annoyed sigh or a sigh of boredom, but a final exhale of breath after the realization that what was started wouldn't be finished. It was an acceptance of defeat. "You know how much I miss you? I stole your perfume so I could smell you when I'm on the cots."

"You're not that far away."

"I know."

He didn't offer an explanation as to why he couldn't sleep at home, or why he'd decided to stay away for days. I was owed that.

"Are you coming home now?" I asked.

"I need to be here."

"You're pushing it, darling."

"I know, baby."

"I'll be at Jenn's opening tomorrow at five. The masks."

"I thought you saw it last week."

"It's been in previews or something. Ask her when you see her. Don't come if you want to sleep in. But if you sleep in, you sleep here."

"Is that an order?"

It shouldn't have to be an order, but I couldn't read him well enough to know if he was being playful or if he was offended at having his leash yanked.

"Consider it an order."

Chapter Eleven

CADEN

There was no starving it while Greyson was in my life. The Thing hovered back in the ambience until I thought of her, then it smiled. When she beeped me, it made its presence known. And when I recognized her voice, I felt it listening.

Leaving her was not an option. Cutting her out wouldn't make me sane any more than pretending the Thing didn't exist would. I needed her. Before her, I had been made of broken glass in a padded bag. Everything looked fine on the outside, but I'd been cutting myself. She opened the bag and put the shards together.

I loved her too much to choose this Thing over her. That much I was sure of. But outside the OR, I couldn't think clearly. Couldn't create a solution or make a decision in the thick swirl of jealousy and panic. Every thought walked a razor's edge between sanity and insanity, and the edge kept moving until I didn't know which side was which.

Every day, it got worse. Even if the Thing wasn't fully present, I felt its pressure against the skin of my mind, pressing against the membrane like a fist punching a latex wall. When I woke in a sweat, the pressure increased, and when she called, it burst through. My emotions were getting sucked into the black hole of this nightmare and I couldn't shake it. The glue got stickier every day.

The treatment wasn't a cure, but I craved it.

It was a perversion.

To quell the Thing, I had to hurt Greyson. I had to fuck her like a fighter. Mark her like a vandal. Break her like a champion.

I could make her come over and over while I did it too. That satisfied every part of me and made the Thing howl. It separated me from it. Severed the tie.

If I could take advantage of that opportunity long enough to talk to her, maybe we could fix this. All I had to do was get over the humiliation of not being in control of my own mind.

I HAD a million excuses to avoid the opening and only one reason to go. The reason was Greyson. So I went.

Seeing my wife in a public place meant I could put off the inevitable long enough to change my mind, chase her away, talk myself into some other course of action. By the time I got there, I had my full mental facilities only by way of making sure my emotions were not engaged.

When I saw her standing in a little black dress and heels, her fingers curved around a wine glass, I felt something.

But desire wasn't an emotion. Possession wasn't an emotion.

I kissed her cheek, and as expected, the Thing jumped into the space between us.

I wasn't angry as much as I wanted to battle it and win.

Combativeness wasn't an emotion either. Or maybe it was. I didn't care.

"Congratulations," I said to Jenn. When I kissed her cheek, I kissed her cheek. No third party slid in on the action.

Tina approached and introduced herself, as expected. I smiled and shook her hand. Same thing as Jenn. Nothing jumped between where we touched.

"I've been wooing your wife," she said. "I hope you don't mind."

"It depends on what kind of wooing you're talking about."

"Professional wooing," Greyson said.

"Did they legalize that?"

Tina laughed. Greyson slapped my arm playfully then looped her hand inside my elbow. The Thing felt good about that but couldn't find a way in through the fabric.

"I hope you don't have to work as hard as I did," I said. "She drives a hard bargain."

Tina clicked my glass. "Thanks for the tip."

"I'm sure no one will have to work as hard as he did," Greyson said.

"Sounds like quite a story." Tina sipped her water.

"Not really," Greyson said. "My unit went to Balad to assist the combat support hospital. I had to assess their fitness—"

"She decided I was unfit."

"I did not!"

"You did." I looked down at her, checking her status. Raised eyebrows. Relaxed mouth.

I wanted to fuck her everywhere. Hard. Later. I would have to. Nothing was getting starved tonight. Not my hunger for her and not the Thing.

She smiled. If I wasn't fooling her into thinking I was all right, I was at least charming her into believing it. Good.

I turned back to Tina. "She said I was overworked. She said I needed rest or I'd make a mistake."

"Which did you do? Rest or make a mistake?"

"Neither."

"Of course," Greyson chimed in. "He beat the odds. It's what he does."

I nodded, satisfied that she thought that. Winners had an easier time winning.

Danny came by. I shook his hand. He kissed my wife in an appropriately platonic manner. "It's like a fucking hospital reunion. I try to get away from you people at night."

"Do your patients know you have such a potty mouth?" I said.

Greyson slipped her hand into mine. I took it away.

"Half of them can't figure out how to use a potty. So no." His orbicularis oris tightened slightly above his left lip. A sneer of a smirk so faint I would have missed it if I wasn't paying attention so coldly. Or maybe that was the reason for the sneer in the first place.

"We're going to look at some masks, if you don't mind," I said.

"Have at it."

I took Greyson to the side where we could see a mask painted blood red and clamped with a vise. The patient's story was typed onto a framed piece of paper next to it, but I was sure I knew it. We slid sideways to the next one. It had been painted by a skilled hand in Islamic geometric patterns.

"This is nice," I said, but had no follow-up. I usually had reasons to like things. I couldn't find one.

"You should see this one over here."

Again, she tried to hold my hand, and again, I took it away.

"Caden."

"Which one? This one?"

"What's happening?"

She had a hand on each of my elbows, but I couldn't look at her. She was too earnest. Too honest. And all I wanted to do was rip that black dress in two and shove my dick inside her. I wanted to fuck her mouth so deep she choked. Get my cock so far up her ass I—

"I think he used a stencil—"

"To us," she said. "What's happening to *us*?"

All I had to do was say, "nothing," but I still couldn't lie.

Both hands in my pants pockets, I bent so only she could hear me. "I want to be fucking you right now."

"No. No, that's not true." Her eyes filled. They sparkled so brightly when she was about to cry. She blinked. One fell.

Reaching inside my jacket, I snapped my handkerchief open and handed it to her.

She didn't take it. It was poison. Electrified. A pat on the shoulder from a clinician. A slap in the face from a stranger. I didn't have the sense or the will to hold her or whisper reassurances, because the Thing was punching through again, and resisting it took everything I had.

She brought her right toe behind her left heel, spun on the balls of her feet for a clean about-face, and forward marched out the door.

I CAUGHT the cab door before she closed it and slid in next to her, barking the 87th Street address to the driver.

"Greyson, listen to me."

"Why were you assisting on a surgery you've led a hundred times?"

I looked at her as if she was crazy, but she wasn't. Not even a little. "Kate was out sick and Eleanor needed me."

"Bullshit."

"You can ask her."

"Are you having an affair?"

"What? With Eleanor?"

"With anyone."

"No!"

"So what is it then?"

I needed to know what she was perceiving without me dropping hints. "What is what?"

"You're the same as you were at the fundraiser, but worse. You're so cold. You won't touch me. It's like you're somewhere else and I can't take it. I *can't take it.*" The last three words rumbled deep in her throat. It was sexy as hell.

I let my desire for her out of its cage, and it filled me like a balloon. I thrust my body in her direction, leveraging myself on the window behind her.

"You're going to take it." I spit the words like a threat. "You're going to take more of it than you ever took before."

She swallowed. The tears dried up, but not the feelings that caused them. "It's not that easy."

"No, it won't be. I promise you that."

I DIDN'T TOUCH her on the cab ride home. I liked watching her squirm. I liked seeing her body's composure fail as I fucked her mind, leaning close to whisper in her ear.

"Look ahead, and don't say a word. Keep your knees apart. The blood is rushing to your clit. Filling it. It's hard. Feel the way your underwear is rubbing against it. When I fuck you, I'm going to be deep enough to push against it."

I had a raging hard-on the whole way home. When we were alone in the foyer behind a locked door, she put her jacket on the hook. Her lips were parted and I'd bet my medical license she was wet.

I let go of everything. My defenses. My armor. My rage. My fear. When I reached for her, I didn't hold her. I took the edges of the neck of her dress and pulled, tearing it open at the center seam.

She gasped. "Stop."

I had to stop. I felt something then. Relief.

I could stop.

She stood with her hands on her breasts, holding the dress up. "What's happening?"

"You wanted me to touch you. I'm going to touch you. I'm going to touch every inch of you. Just me, my dick, my mouth, you, your mouth, your ass, your tits. I'm leaving nothing on the table."

"There's no one else?" Her arms relaxed and the dress fell a little.

"No. Never."

"Why do you get like this? Like tonight? Like a few weeks ago?"

"Because I need this."

That wasn't a lie, but it wasn't the whole truth. I couldn't think about the whole truth. Not with her torn dress and her pheromones invading my mind.

"Take it."

She let her dress drop. Black lace bra. Garter. Stockings. A ribbon of underwear. She must have been expecting something tonight.

Oh, how the Thing screamed incoherently when it saw my intentions. How it quivered in fear and impotence.

I undid my belt.

"Nervous?" I asked, taking out my cock.

"A little."

"If you say stop, I stop."

She nodded.

I grabbed her, pressing her body to mine, mouthing her cheek, her lips, her throat, her ear. I nipped her shoulder but didn't bite. Not yet. The Thing was there in the connection, but it was scared.

I pushed her to her knees.

"Open." I squeezed her cheeks and put my dick in it, pushing deep past her gag reflex. "Come on. Take it."

When I pushed again, she opened her throat.

The Thing wept, but wasn't scared away. Not yet. Not when I fucked her face or grabbed a fistful of hair to guide her rhythm. Not when I came in her mouth and it dripped from the corner of her lips.

I helped her stand and kissed her hard, tasting bitter cum on her tongue. "Upstairs."

I watched her go, gartered ass waving as she climbed. Alone for a second at the base of the stairs, I put my hand on the bannister to steady myself.

"You ready?" I whispered. "I'm going to fuck her so hard you disappear forever."

For the second time, the ambient hush of its voice made words.

I'll never leave her.

"We'll see about that."

SHE WAS SITTING on the edge of the bed with her hands folded between her knees. The part of me that I'd let loose, the emotion and uncertainty, wanted to take her right there. But I didn't. I had another piece, a cold, calculating piece. He was more methodical.

She watched me undress and put my clothes on the chair.

I stood in front of her, already erect as a fucking flagpole. "You're the only one, Greyson."

Her brown eyes were sad, open, honest. I couldn't comfort her. Not now.

"You're different sometimes."

"I know."

I pushed her down and jerked her legs open. I could smell her sweet pussy through the strip of underwear. I ripped them open. She tried to get up on her elbows, but I pushed down on her chest, leaning my weight on her as I put two fingers deep in her cunt.

"Get your knees up. Show me everything."

She did it, and the Thing's rage and sadness mixed with desire.

"You're so fucking wet for it." I rubbed her until my fingers were lubricated, then I stuck them in her ass.

The Thing ran from between the place we touched as if it was burned.

"Oh, God," she cried.

We'd had anal sex before. Gentle, slow anal. I couldn't guarantee this would be either.

I held her down and twisted my fingers deep inside her. "Beg for it."

"Please, Caden. Fuck me. Please."

"Where?"

"My pussy."

I flipped her over and yanked her to the edge of the bed until her toes were on the floor. Then I wiped my fingers on the handkerchief she'd refused earlier.

I couldn't believe what I was about to do.

No. I could. The Thing couldn't.

She saw me hesitate. "What are you doing?"

Holding her arms together behind her back, I kicked her legs wide open. "Say stop if you want me to."

"I just want to know."

I slapped her ass. She yelped.

I expected the whirlwind with the shredding of another boundary, but it didn't show.

Gripping her arms hard, I hit her bottom hard enough to leave a red mark. "Where do you want me to fuck you?"

"My pussy."

Slap. And again, harder. She yelled again, wiggling.

"Here's a hint." Four fingers gathered moisture, circling her cunt. She rotated with me. "It's not this."

Three fingers in her ass. She tightened down.

The Thing was in deep distress. It felt so good to beat it, but there was no whirlwind. I needed it. I didn't know what it did or why it was important, but without the second of spinning confusion, the Thing wouldn't hide completely.

I took her by the throat. The winds appeared and waited, like gods called by an offering.

"Beg," I demanded.

"Fuck my ass, Caden. Take it."

I tightened my grip on her neck. "You want four fingers in your ass?"

"Please! Please put your cock in my ass."

"Good girl."

I took her cunt instead.

She made a sound between a gasp and a grunt.

Letting her arms go, I pulled the lube from the night table drawer and let it fall from her back to her crack as I fucked her.

"You want to come?"

"Yes."

"Later." I pulled out and slid the head of my cock along her ass.

She was nervous. I didn't want her to be nervous, but the whirlwind spun into my perception, whispering promises.

"Breathe."

She nodded.

"Inhale," I continued.

She did. I watched the four-inch scar on her chest rise to expand with the air, and on the exhale, I slid inside her, watching her pucker expand into an O around the head. Maneuvering myself deeper, I stretched her into a tight ring around my shaft. Her face contorted in pain.

I stopped.

The Thing was still there, confused, using my love as a vulnerability.

The centrifuge slowed, waiting.

I pulled out and turned her over, pulling her knees up. She exposed herself willingly, and the love I'd been hiding was nearly crushed by the spinning in my mind.

She pulled her cheeks apart, mouthing, "Fuck me."

That was it. I didn't need to be told twice, but I needed to take more than was offered. Mercilessly, I took her ass with every inch, burying myself in her.

She closed her eyes.

"Beg or say stop," I said.

"Please. Take it."

I put her hand between her legs. She circled her clit. I slid all the way in, burying myself in her. Wrapping my arm around her, I put my weight on the base of her throat, just above her sternum, until she was immobile.

I spun, a slave to my sickness, flipping from the man I was to the man I am.

To ring that throat.

To hold her high.

To own her completely.

I lost it. In a swirl of me, her, my love, my control, and the Thing I couldn't name, screaming out and away.

Chapter Twelve

GREYSON

I had bruises on my left wrist where he'd held me down. He had been more gentle with the right side, which had never really recovered from the break I got in basic training, but the left took what was left over. I couldn't let patients see it.

The first time he fucked me with brutality, we didn't talk about it. I woke up thinking he'd been half asleep and it wouldn't occur again. Three weeks after that, he'd done it again, pushing me harder, demanding more, taking me to the edge over and over.

Last night, two weeks after the last time, he did it again. He'd fucked me in the ass, in the shower afterward, on the floor. He'd been rough, and the rougher he got, the more I came.

I wanted him to push me hard. I liked it. But this was slipping out of control.

There's a name for this.

It was spring. Long sleeves would be too hot, and the AC in the office was spotty. I rummaged in my drawer and found a loose coil of bracelets. I slid them over my bruised left wrist. That would have to do.

I checked myself in the mirror. I looked fine. No one could see the bruises or the soreness between my legs. No one could see the aches or the pleasant, peaceful satisfaction. Looking at me, you'd never know I'd had my fourth orgasm of the night with my husband's massive cock buried in my throat and four of his fingers inside me.

Masochist.

The word shot through my mind, and for the first time, I let it. I mouthed it in the mirror.

Masochist.

"Where are you off to today?" he asked from the bathroom doorway, arms crossed over his bare chest. His pajama bottoms hung low on his hips, the waistband cutting across the V-shaped indent of his pelvis.

"Collecting data for the Tina thing." I leaned over the vanity and put on lipstick.

"Are you okay? From last night?"

"Uh-huh. Are you?" I snapped the tube closed.

"Yeah." His nod was serious. It was not an enthusiastic agreement as much as a simple affirmative.

"You seem more animated."

His arms unfolded. I'd startled him. "Animated? What's that mean?"

I faced him. "The coldness is gone." I put my hand on his chest and drew it through the patch of hair in the center, down to his abdomen. "Is something going on you want to talk about?"

"No."

I shrugged. I wouldn't normally gesture like that any more than I'd roll my eyes. Normally, I'd acknowledge his feelings without validating or dismissing them. But I didn't feel normal. I felt a little less in control, a little more impulsive. Less like a professional psychiatrist and more like a wife who knew her husband's boundaries.

"You on call today?" I asked.

"Yeah." He took my hand and kissed inside the wrist. "I'll call you."

I kissed him in typical married-person way. A punctuation between activity. A comma in the day. I didn't get to the bedroom door before his voice stopped me.

"Greyson."

"Yeah?"

"I can't take this back once I say it."

This couldn't be good. Anything he might want to take back wouldn't be a statement to celebrate.

"Okay?"

"You might want to cancel your appointment."

"Caden. Is everything all right?"

Sucking his lips between his teeth as if he wanted to hold the words back, he tightened his jaw and tilted his head. We were frozen in his moment of decision while the currents of his courage swirled and gathered together.

"I think." Hands though hair. A pause. I stayed absolutely still. "I think I'm going crazy."

Part Two

HOMEBREAKING

Chapter Thirteen

GREYSON - DECEMBER, 2006

Caden's hands, what they could do, how careful they were in doing it, were always different in my memory than in real life. I forgot them every time they were out of my sight. They were always wider, more articulated than I remembered. When I saw his wedding ring on the fourth finger, tying him to me, I stood in awe of that single band taming a force so powerful.

"Hey," he said, meeting me at the desk at the front of the administrative offices of the hospital. He was crisp and showered in a suit with a textured silk tie. He always smelled of alcohol when he got out of surgery. He covered it with cologne and sex, but it was deep in his pores.

When he signed out, his gold ring wiggled with the letters of his name.

"How are you feeling? Since this morning?" I asked, remembering the taste of those fingers.

"If I wasn't fine, I'd let you know," he lied.

I let him have that particular deceit because it was to protect me. He was painfully honest in everything else. We started down the hall.

When my heels clacked on the floor, he looked at my feet. "Are you all right in those?"

I turned my calf so he could see the outline of the shoe and the stockings under it. "Do you like them?"

He walked again. "I like them over my shoulders."

Stating facts. Clear and concise. Cold because he was nervous, not because he was losing his mind. He wasn't lying about feeling better, only that he'd tell me.

"How's your thigh?" he asked when we were alone in the elevator.

"Nice contusion."

"Muscular or dermal?"

"Subcutaneous."

He nodded, hands folded together in front of him. "I'll be more careful next time."

We got out at the doctors' level of the garage, which was nicer than any of the others, and had valet. His Mercedes was waiting. He let me in.

"Where are we meeting him again?" he asked.

"Gotham."

"We should have taken a cab."

The car pulled onto Central Park West. It was the week between Christmas and New Year. Traffic was on a break.

"It was a cutting day," I said with a playful curl to my question. Surgery left him raw and potent. We usually fucked on cutting days.

"Just a quad. Easy. He was young though. So we had tertiary distress."

He made a left, crossing hand over hand, his attention always sharp, even when the streets were empty.

"You don't want to go," I said.

"To dinner?"

"To dinner with Ronin."

"I like Ronin."

"To dinner with Ronin to discuss the new protocol."

"No." He faced me when he made the denial, and for a second, I saw his raw power. "I don't want to go to dinner with Ronin to discuss this at all. Ever."

"You don't have to."

"Yes, I do, Greyson."

"You *don't*."

"Yes. I. Do. For you."

"Don't lay this on me."

"Jesus Christ. If I wrote you a check for three hundred bucks, would you listen to me for fifty minutes? We're married. I do things for you. You do things for me. We make sacrifices."

Before I could talk about agency, autonomy, and acceptance, he grabbed my hand and squeezed it. For a month, his touch outside our home had gotten rare, and it froze me.

When I squeezed back, he put his hand back on the wheel to pull the car up to the valet. My fingers were left alone to make their own sense of him.

THE HOSTESS LED us through the cavernous space. Pillars of changing light held up the thirty-foot ceiling, and the sounds of conversations and music were muffled by careful acoustics. Caden put his hand on my lower back to guide me through, and I kept pace in six-inch heels.

Ronin had finished basic and been stationed in Maryland. He wouldn't say where, but I knew it was the Aberdeen Proving Ground. He knew I knew and neither confirmed nor denied what he did for a living.

He was alone at a table in the corner, reading a magazine. In the folds, I saw half of President Bush's face. He stood when we approached.

"Colonel," Caden said.

"St. John," he replied, shaking Caden's hand first.

I envied the public touch, then I gave my own handshake and let Caden pull my seat out for me. We ordered drinks. Wine for me. Whiskey for Ronin. Water for Caden.

Ronin had been a handsome man in basic training, but his eyes had matured from simply piercing to devastating, and his conceit had ripened into confidence.

"We haven't seen you since the fundraiser," I said. "Are you still with that girl?"

He leaned back to let the waitress place the glass of whiskey in front of him. "Nah."

"I'm sorry to hear it."

"Not a big deal. It takes a certain type to deal with me." His eyes met mine, then Caden's, and he smirked. He asked about Caden's residency, my feelings about private practice. Usually we wouldn't ask about his job, but this time was different.

"I mentioned we wanted to talk to you about something specific," I started.

"You had me at 'secret.'"

The waitress came and took our order. It took forever to hear the specials. I didn't have much of an appetite, even though I hadn't eaten all day. I needed the feeling of being at a peak of tolerance.

"To old friends," Ronin held up his drink, and we clicked.

Caden looked as if he'd rather be cut into small pieces than sit at that table.

"So," I said, "I'll get right to the point."

"Please," Caden said.

I leaned toward Ronin. "I hear Aberdeen was working on a heightened sensory perception protocol?"

Ronin made no sign he was surprised. "I'm sure I don't know what you're talking about."

"To increase the accuracy of scopaesthesia. The feeling you're being watched."

"He knows what scopaesthesia is."

I ignored my husband. "For troops on the front line. If they can perceive when they're being watched, they can kill first."

Ronin leaned back, crossing his legs while he fingered his glass. "And this is interesting to you because?"

I looked at Caden, and he looked at me. This was the moment we broke the shell we'd grown around ourselves. For me. For us.

"Caden has a persistent condition."

Back to Caden. He wasn't looking at me. He was touching his water glass with his left hand, and that ring, those fingers, the way the index finger tapped once.

"He thinks someone's watching him."

"Not watching," Caden cuts in. "It's not malicious."

"It's trying to get inside him."

Ronin uncrossed his legs. "That sounds pretty malicious."

"It's—"

Caden put his cold fingers on my arm, and I stopped. "It wants to join with me. I don't have a feeling it wants to hurt me. It is, just so you know, crazy. It's not normal. It's fucking insane crazy talk and I'm embarrassed to be sitting here telling you about it."

"Having a wife will do that to you."

They shared a male moment and I let it slide.

"So," Ronin continued, "you've checked environmental causes?"

"Had the house checked for carbon monoxide," he said.

"And you've considered PTSD? I mean, your wife's a card-carrying expert."

"It's not PTSD," I interjected.

"Really? You were in Fallujah. Anyone who didn't go crazy already was."

We sat in a triangle of silence with our own memories of the blood, the screaming, the smell of gunpowder and meat. The food came. I was sure it smelled great to a person who was interested in eating. None of us were. When the waitress asked if we wanted anything else, no one answered.

I broke the silence. "It's not PTSD. No flashbacks. No disrupted sleep. No emotional outbursts."

No emotion at all. I didn't say that. It wasn't relevant, and it wasn't one hundred percent true.

"It's a nascent dissociative disorder," I continued.

"Wait, wait, wait..." Ronin threw up his hands.

"It's not—" Caden tried to get a word in.

"Have you tried antipsychotics even?"

"Yes," I said. "We've tried everything. But every few weeks, the feeling comes back. We get it under control, but it's been every week, and now it's every five days or so. It used to be every few months, but last time, we had a four-day spread."

Ronin looked from me to Caden, then back to me, twisting his hands out to show us his palms. "You do *what* to get it under control?"

I couldn't answer, and Caden wouldn't. Instead he said, "I need this protocol. We do. We need it now."

"What. Do. You. Do?" Ronin planted his flag in the ground.

Caden plucked it out by putting his elbows on the table and locking his gaze on our friend. "I fuck Greyson so hard I hurt her."

"Jesus." Ronin drained his whiskey.

"I gain control of her body and all of it goes away."

"Is this a control thing or a sadism thing?"

Trust Ronin to get right to the point.

"I don't know. But one day, I'm going to really injure her."

"No, you're not," I insisted, but I was background noise. It was all Caden now.

"Whatever this is," he continued, "it's not telling me to kill the neighbor's dog. It's not a schizoid hallucination channeling my id. It's a separate thing. It's not just distracting, it's overwhelming, and you know me. Right? You know I don't spook."

Ronin nodded. He'd been with us in Fallujah. He knew what Caden could do in the face of death. He'd seen how, when necessary, ice water flowed through my husband's veins.

"You do not spook," he confirmed.

"We need this," I said.

"I'm not saying I know what you're talking about, but let's say I did. Let's say I knew a way to heighten your feelings, including feelings of being watched. What then? It'll only make it worse."

"Only if it's real," I replied. "It heightens the feeling of real eyes. A real enemy. Caden isn't on the battlefield. There's no enemy. This could shake the entire thing loose. Ronin." I put my hand over his. "Please. Send me the efficacy report and I'll look at it with an open mind. If I think it won't help, I'll drop it."

He took his hand away and used it to hold up his empty

whiskey glass for the server. He snapped his napkin open and draped it over his lap, then slid his fork off the table. "Ten bucks says this isn't even pink inside."

Caden picked up his steak knife. "You wouldn't know pink if you had your face in it."

I wasn't finished with the conversation, but they were. I picked up my fork and poked at my salad. I felt as if I'd gone to battle and suddenly, without reason, everyone had laid down arms and gone home for lunch with the wounded still bleeding into the mud.

AFTER SEEING RONIN AT GOTHAM, Caden and I were under the sheets in a warm bed, watching the shadows of leaves dance on the ceiling. I knew he wasn't sleeping, and he had to be aware that I was awake.

"Was it hard to tell Ronin?" I asked finally.

"Yes."

"We have to try everything at this point."

"I know. But I don't have to like it."

I turned my body toward his and draped my arm over his chest. "One day, we'll look back on this and say it was the greatest adventure of our lives."

"We're not making happy memories."

"They'll be different when they're in the rearview."

He turned to face me. His nose was a quarter inch from mine, and he might as well have been in a different room. "This won't. Not for me."

"Let's see. Give it time."

"I'm not even in my own skin. Do you know what it's like to have a brain that's not doing what it's supposed to do?"

"No."

"I'm a stranger to myself. It's torture. It's like I'm broken. Ripped up. And I can't find the wound to stitch up. When I hurt you, it's like I find it for a little while, but a new one opens. I've never been afraid before. Not really. But when it gets bad and I feel it coming, I don't know what I'm going to do to stop it, or what's going to happen if it takes me over."

I kissed him. "It won't. We have everything we need to figure it out."

"You've been saying that for months."

"It's still true. I don't give up."

"Don't give up on me, Major One More."

"Never. I'll never give up on you."

We shifted like tectonic plates, fitting the muscles and bones of our bodies together until we found comfort in the way our shapes clicked and fell asleep in each other's arms.

Chapter Fourteen

CADEN - SEPTEMBER, 2001

I was at a prestigious residency at NYU Medical Center, learning under the best heart surgeon on the planet. Roberto García had performed over two thousand open heart procedures, and he'd taken me under his wing. Everything was going fine.

On September 11th, 2001, that all fell apart.

I was on the morning shift when I was called down to emergency. Caked in filth, encased in equipment, burned, screaming, the horror of it all revealed in bones and blood. I wasn't training as an ER surgeon, but they needed me, so I became one. The nurses were spectacular. They helped me get a handle on the sudden situation. I locked off any feelings about what was happening while I did the job.

Between crises, I tried to call my parents. The cellular lines were jammed. No one was getting through. There was talk of other cities. Other planes. The entire system was shut down. Nothing flying. Nothing landing.

The world was chaos, but inside myself, I did what I had to. I cut. I sewed. I made decisions. For twenty-four insane hours, I was order inside madness.

A nurse named Lola dumped a bag of ice into the metal sink and turned on the water.

"Thank you," I said, but she was already gone.

The parade of casualties had slowed, but no one had time for niceties when the world was falling apart. My eyes were burning. My knees were painfully swollen. When the sink was full, I stuck my head in it. The cold shocked my mind clear.

When I pulled my head out of the ice water, someone put a towel in my hands. I assumed it was Lola, but then he spoke with his deep Mexican accent.

"Stay still."

Fingers on the inside of my wrist.

"I'm fine, Roberto."

He didn't answer while he counted. The bright fluorescents had a density all their own, and the sage green of the tile walls was loud against the soft blues of the linoleum floor. Outside the scrub room, staff ran past the windows. I needed to help them.

"You're tachy," he said, letting go of my wrist. "But better than I expected."

I ran the towel through my hair. Dr. García was five foot five with a head of thick black hair. He had the wide cheeks and full lips of his Mixtec ancestors.

"I'm fine. How many are in triage?"

"You need to rest."

"I told you I was fine."

"No one bathes in ice water when they're fine." I was about to argue, but he cut me off. "Go take a nap before I write you up. And then we're going to talk about your future."

He had the power to fail me out. He wouldn't, but I was tired and my face must have registered shock or disappointment, because he responded.

"You're too good at this, St. John. Cardiac surgery is a waste of your talent."

"What? Wait."

My beeper went off, startling me. I tilted it to see the grey-and-black screen. It was my parents' house, but not the code they used for emergencies.

"My mother."

"We can talk next week." García said, snapping the towel out of my hands. He tossed the towel into the hamper on his way out.

I flipped open my phone and called her. For the first time in dozens of tries, it connected.

"Caden."

It wasn't my mother.

"Who is this?"

"It's Kent. I'm your father's financial advisor twenty years now."

I scanned my memory. I'd met him. Business dinners at the house. Holiday cocktails. He'd tried to get me to buy term life insurance. "Why are you in my parents' house?"

"I have all the keys..."

"Where's my mother?" I recognized the hum of the refrigerator in the background, but only when it clicked off.

"I called from my number, but you weren't picking up." Kent Whoever had a desperate edge to his voice.

"I asked you a question. Where's my mother?"

Someone else murmured in my kitchen.

"We don't know," Kent said. "We were wondering if you'd seen them."

"*We?*" I didn't know why I latched onto the pronoun. Nothing could have been less important, but that was the most comprehensible straw to grasp, because as far as I was concerned, my father was somewhere in the city, sewing people back together, and my mother was home, on 87th Street, far away from the fallen towers.

More murmurs from my kitchen. Their kitchen. The kitchen I thought of when I thought of home. I was ten steps behind, still wrestling with taking a nap or demanding Garcia tell me what the fuck he meant about my future.

"My... we..." Kent shook the shit out of his head. "It doesn't matter. I have... I *had* an office in the North Tower."

I don't care why is he telling me this why isn't he dead but he's in the house...

"And I was late," Kent continued. "But your parents were on time."

"Of course they were on fucking time." I snapped up this lonely coherent straw, but that was the last one I'd get. "And you were late, so you're in their house calling me to tell me what?"

"Have you heard from them since the attack?"

"No. The lines are jammed."

"There's no need to panic."

"I'm not panicked, Kent."

"There are posters all over the city."

I hadn't been outside the hospital in thirty hours. Something was happening. Something inky black, dropping into my clear mind, was curling into the calm waters, wider and wider. Soon, there would be no discrete color in the solution. "I have no idea what you're talking about."

"Can you check admitting lists?"

"For—"

—*who?*

The reality of the world clicked with the state of my little life. My parents. Kent's office. The call from their house. I knew who I was checking the other hospitals' lists for, and I knew why.

"Yes. I'll take care of it." I knew how to do that. I had it under control, and if I wanted to keep it that way, I had to make it a point to look forward, not down. If I looked down, I'd be afraid to fall. "Don't worry," I said to him, but really, to me. "I'll call you if I hear anything."

"Thank you," he said. "You were always a good kid."

I hung up and let myself have hope. A shining light of a dream the good kid always had, but kept to himself because it was uncomfortable.

I hoped that my father was dead and my mother was alive.

JANUARY, 2007

RONIN'S experimental bullshit wouldn't come up until we were out of options.

The day after Jenn's gallery opening, when I told Greyson I thought I was going crazy, she canceled two morning sessions.

Before we sat down, I'd considered a dozen things I could claim I wanted to talk to her about. Moving out of New York. Having a baby. Divorce. Anything. I would rather have made up a story about cheating on her than admit I was convinced I was being stalked by a... what? Force? Entity? Ghost? Demon? A rogue piece of my own mind? And that after pushing her limits the first time, this Thing had disappeared, only to resurface until I bent her over a banquet table?

It was insane.

But I stood at the kitchen island, across from her seat, and pretended I was someone else. I said it. All of it. The way the Thing folded into the shadows and laced itself inside sounds. The pressure to get rid of it. The raging jealousy the more I sensed it wanted her. The method I'd used to get rid of it twice.

"And you're okay now? Right now?"

"Yes."

"Why didn't you tell me yesterday?"

"I didn't want to tell you in front of it."

She nodded, finishing her tea, thinking for a long time.

I hadn't wanted to tell her, and even though that last admission was the craziest, it had come more easily than the first because of who she was. Greyson accepted me at face value. She listened. Always. If she thought I was losing my mind, she didn't show it. There was no judgment in her.

Thank God for her. A lesser woman would have done so much more damage.

Finally, she spoke. "I think your reaction is very sane."

"My reaction to losing my mind?"

"Those types of phrases aren't helpful."

"Let's not do this."

"Do what?"

"I need you to not be a psychiatrist about it."

She brought her teacup to the sink. "That's hard. But all right. I won't monitor your words."

"Thank you."

"So obviously it's a form of PTSD. Is it affecting your work?"

"Not at all."

"How is that possible?" She got a notepad from a drawer and plucked a pencil from a cup of them.

"Compartmentalization, baby."

She smiled and leaned her hip against the counter with her pencil hovering over the paper. "Sure. All right. When did this start?"

I took the pencil and pad away and put them aside. "You're not doing an intake form on me."

"It helps me think if I write it down."

I gathered her in my arms and kissed her neck. "But it makes me uncomfortable. I only want to tell my wife."

She exhaled deeply in my arms. "When did it start?"

"It started soon after you got back, but I think it's been with me the whole time. Since the war. I brought it back from Iraq."

"Are you sure?"

I let her go.

"Could it be September eleventh?" she asked.

I sat on the stool and faced her, letting our legs tangle between us. "I wasn't exactly looking for it. So I don't know."

"And what is it like, this Thing?"

"It's... inside things. I hear it in ambient noise and in the shadows."

"In your peripheral vision?"

"No. Looking straight at it or not, it's there. Sometimes there's nothing to see, but I know it's there."

"Hm. So it's an it, not a who?"

"It's not a person, but it has a personality."

"Can you describe it?"

I laughed a little at myself. "I know there's no intake form, but man, it seems like there is."

"Please?" She ran her hands down my arms, giving her plea a warmth and need she wouldn't have given a patient.

"It's nice."

"Nice?"

"It's a nice personality. Not charming or interesting. Compassionate. Gentle. Kindhearted. The only person in the world it hates is me."

"Why?"

"Because you're mine. Every time you're in the room, it gets stronger. Every time I think of you, it comes out a little more." I pressed my lips together and breathed deeply. "It's making me not want to think of you, and that's unacceptable. Trying to keep away from you? I thought I could starve it out, but if I starve it out, I starve you out. I won't let it do that to me."

I laid her palm on mine. Her nails were short and clean. Unpolished, yet delicate.

"I stuff all my feelings away, because it feeds on them. You'd be sick to your stomach if you knew how easy it is for me to do that. It gets easier every day, and when I can't anymore, I fuck you hard because it hates that. It hides so it doesn't have to watch. Then there's this spinning sensation, like my mind is being flipped and spun... then it's gone until next time."

She put her hand on my face. I kissed her palm.

"I'm sorry," I said. "You didn't know you were marrying into this mess."

"Neither did you."

"I wouldn't want to go through it with anyone else, but at the same time, I'm sorry it's you. You deserve better."

"And you deserve the best, which is me." She smiled and waggled her brows.

I laughed but cut it off. She meant it to be funny, but I wasn't ready to laugh about this.

"Do you have to wait to hurt me? Wait until you're all bottled up and stone-faced?"

"I don't know. I haven't tried it."

She slid off the stool. "Do you feel it now? The Thing? So close after you chased it away?"

"It's there but hiding. I can manage it."

"Hurt me now," she said thickly.

When I'd hurt her before, I was under the influence of whatever this sickness was. I could only see one path out, and it was through her pain. Any other time, it wouldn't be right.

"Greyson." I ran my fingers along her throat, feeling the bend of her tendons under soft skin. "I can't."

"Yes, you can." She put her lips to my cheek. "Hurt me."

Her whisper turned my compassion into sex. I turned my mouth to her throat and bit it.

"Harder."

I bit harder, sucking apples off her skin. She gasped. Her face tightened. She pushed my face into her throat, and I sucked and bit her, grabbing her by the waist, pulling skin between my teeth.

She groaned, and I tasted blood. I pulled away. A red spot had formed inside deep, tooth-shaped indents. Her brown eyes were wide and her pupils were dilated.

"Are you all right?" I asked.

She put her hand to her new wound. "Yeah, I'm... did it go away?"

It had been faint before. I gave it my attention, feeling in the corners and behind the hiss of the water heater. "It's there. Same as before."

"Maybe you have to be fucking me?"

"It starts screaming and hiding before that. And I'd like to fuck you right now." I put my hand up her shirt and found her nipple.

The red marks on her neck were getting brighter and angrier as blood flowed to the site. Seeing the mark made my blood flow as well. I'd done that, and painfully. She was mine. I pinched her nipple, watching her suck in a breath. I twisted it, and her eyelids fluttered.

Drawing my hands down her sides, I pushed her pants down. "Let me make you come."

Before she could answer, I got two fingers on her clit and her reply turned into a groan. I guided one hand to the stool behind her and the other to the counter. She locked her left elbow and curved her back, thrusting her hips toward me.

"Would you stop if I said no?" I rotated my fingers on her nub, watching her try to maintain control over her questions. "While we're doing it and you were hurting me? If I said stop, could you?"

We were down to calling roughness and domination "it." I doubted Greyson missed the way we glossed it over when we weren't in the moment.

"Probably." I got two fingers into her, then drew them back over her clit so wet I barely had to touch it.

"I need something... I'm so close... more definite."

Increasing the pressure, I brought her to the next level but reduced it to keep her on the edge. "I could."

"Then we should keep doing it."

"You like it."

"I do. I do. God, let me come."

Wiggling back under her shirt, I pinched her nipple again. This time, I made sure it hurt. Not for the Thing, which was too far away to perceive it, but because I couldn't believe what she'd said until I tested it with a loving heart.

But it was true. She threw her head back and rotated her hips against me. Her clit was bloated and tight with blood. The harder I pinched her nipple, the more the pain kept her from going over the edge into orgasm. She hovered in my hand, under my control with no more than a few fingers.

"I'm going to let you come."

"Yes. Please."

I slowly increased the pressure on her clit, circling it with her rhythm until she arched her back, leaning on her left arm, stiffening over my hand. She let out an *unh*, then jerked away so forcefully her hair fell over her face. Her chest heaved.

"Thank you," she said breathlessly, pushing the hair off her face.

"My pleasure." I sucked the end of a slick finger.

She put her hands on my shoulders and pressed her body between my legs. "I have the rest of the morning off."

"I don't." I kissed her and stood. "So we'll reconvene tonight."

"I'm going to call some people then."

"Okay." I untangled myself from her and pushed the stools in.

"Would you like a man or a woman?"

"Excuse me?"

"Therapist."

"Whoa, there."

"You need to work with someone else. Another professional. I can't manage your treatment."

I hadn't regretted telling her until she suggested a stranger, but how could I be surprised? And how could I have avoided telling her? She was my wife and the target of my... whatever it was. Logically, I couldn't have avoided this shitty situation. I knew it, but I didn't have to like it.

"No."

"Caden. Please."

"You want me, a surgeon, to tell someone about this and expect them to let me continue working?"

"It's not affecting your work."

"I need to work. So no."

"I won't treat you. Period." She crossed her arms. "I mean it. It's not some arbitrary limit, because believe me, my instinct is to be your primary advocate. I'd step in front of anything for you. But I know, in the end, that won't serve you." She put her hands flat on my chest. "You're everything to me. Everything. I'm too invested."

Looking down at her, parallel lines of straight hair filtering one brown eye, the strands caught in her dark lashes, I accepted her love. Her professionalism was fine, but when she said she was doing it for me, I believed her.

"I don't want to tell anyone else about this. Who's not going to think I'm crazy?"

"Anyone in the field."

"I'm not going on a hundred interviews."

"I'll find you someone right away. It'll be easy."

I kissed her temple. "All right." I held her tight, resting my chin on her head.

"We're going to be all right," she said. "I promise."

"So do I."

Chapter Fifteen

Most non-medicinal PTSD treatments focus on desensitizing the patient to the trauma itself. They relive it endless times via sensory stimulation or verbal recall, until it's old news. The therapies can seem cruel, but the outcomes are consistently good.

Caden wouldn't take medication. You can educate a man out of his misinterpretations of data (these drugs do not effect one's ability to perform surgery) but you cannot educate him out of his pride (tell that to the person on the table).

As terrible patients went, he would be the absolute worst.

"How did it go?" I asked from my desk one afternoon in early December. He'd called me after seeing another PTSD specialist.

"Fine."

"Did you like him?"

"I don't know. I was only there fifteen minutes."

"Why?" I asked.

"I was late. Anyway, he wants to identify a specific trauma. I don't have a specific trauma."

"That may take work but—"

"I have to go."

"Okay. I love you."

"I love you too." He hung up.

I stared at the plastic receiver as if that would keep us connected another moment, then I put it back in the cradle with a sigh.

Since he'd told me about what he called the Thing three weeks earlier, I'd defined behaviors that had seemed free-floating before. In the days before the fundraiser, he'd been cold and emotionless. He was so detached and robotic in some ways, yet temperamental and snippy in others. After the dark banquet room, where he dominated my body so brutally I had to hide his bite mark for a week, he was back to almost normal. Not as normal as when I met him in Iraq, but you get what you get and you don't get upset.

As the weeks passed, he became more and more closed off. There had been three-plus weeks between the first rough encounter in the middle of the night and the banquet hall. I thought nothing of the timing except to note when he'd become alienated from his emotions.

I was about to call the next therapist on my list when Jenn called.

"I need a drink," she said.

I looked at my watch. It was five thirty already. "I've had seven sessions today and my brain is full."

"Meet you downstairs."

THAT WAS the mood I met Jenn in.

That was how it began, really. Ronin and his classified secrets, breaking shit to fix it.

Caden had paperwork and opted not to join Jenn and me. Good. I was frustrated with him even though it wasn't his fault. Never get frustrated with the patient, even if he's your husband, slowing down before we got to a dead end. I wanted to speed up and find out what that wall was really made of.

I was relieved he didn't want to come, and then guilty for wanting a reprieve from watching him go through the motions of life.

Jenn pushed her glasses up her nose. She'd shaved her kinky black hair down to the skin, which made her features statuesque. She held up her beer glass. I clinked my wine.

"To an empty brain," she said.

"Cheers."

The Wednesday crowd was subdued. The Wall Street douches had had a bad day apparently, and the art school kids huddled over pitchers of the cheap stuff.

"So," I said. "You know anyone who can see a vet about identifying a trauma?"

"What about Warren?"

"I need someone to ID the incident so we can do CPT with Warren or whomever." Cognitive Processing Therapy was a simple reliving of the trauma, but if the patient wasn't sure what exactly had happened, or was in denial that a trauma had occurred, that was a different kettle of fish.

"Messy. What are the symptoms?"

"Patient thinks he's being watched."

"Oh, shit! I have to tell you something." She leaned forward on her elbows. "This is apropos of nothing. Ronin's working at Blackthorne Solutions."

I should have told her no right there. Should have said I didn't want anything to do with his crazy bullshit.

Instead, I raised my eyebrows and put on a face that said, "Tell me more."

"I got a test subject request from Aberdeen for symptoms relating to... check this out... a feeling of being watched." She pinched her fingers together at her forehead and spread them out, letting them flutter as they moved away from her head.

"And this leads to Ronin how?"

"It was an old form and his name was still on it."

"So he was working on that when he left?"

"I think so. Do you want the form?"

"Maryland's not an option."

"But Ronin's here..." she singsonged. "You could see what he's got going at Blackthorne."

"No."

I was too quick to deny. Blackthorne was a military contractor that took payment from governments and corporations. They sent security personnel into war zones, used mercenaries and special operators to manage power vacuums in small countries, and developed weapons for the Pentagon.

I didn't want the form, but if I really did have a patient like Caden, I'd get it.

"I mean, maybe." I changed my answer.

"Let me know."

We moved to other topics. She asked how my proposal from Tina was coming. I asked about art therapy and the NEA. We didn't talk about Blackthorne or my patient again, but I didn't stop thinking about it. Even after I found someone for Caden and he got his ass on a couch for a session, I made sure I had an updated number for Ronin.

CADEN HADN'T WANTED to meet Ronin for dinner. Hadn't wanted to tell him a damn thing. Didn't like him or trust him. But we were out of options, and he knew it.

When we got home from Gotham, Caden silently helped me with my coat. His fists were tight and his eyes burned. His muscles were taut under his shirt, and he smelled of need. My body reacted by sending a flood of fluid from my mouth, which had gone utterly dry, to my crotch, which was suddenly dripping.

"Greyson," he said.

He reached around me and flipped the deadbolt, then stepped away enough to frame the whole of my body in his sight. His eyes coursed over my edges and curves while he flexed his fingers.

"How do you feel?" I asked.

No answer.

"Now? Is it the Thing?"

"Yes."

"Okay." I started unbuttoning my blouse, helpless against the smile creeping across my face.

"Say yes." His fingers went from flex to fist over and over as if he was stopping himself from using them.

"Yes."

I undid the second button but never got to the third before he ripped the shirt open, sending buttons flying. He pushed me against the wall, hand under my bra, squeezing my breast.

He shoved his other hand under my skirt and found my wetness. "That's right, baby."

I was pushed down onto my knees with my bra over my tits and my skirt half over my waist. He undid his jeans and pulled his cock out like a weapon. A drop glistened at the tip.

Pushing the back of my head forward, he guided himself into my mouth. "Take all of it. And make it wet. You're going to need it."

I opened my throat and let him fuck my mouth. Spit dripped from my lower lip. I groaned, vibrating for him when he was deep in me. He came down my throat and watched as I swallowed.

Looking up at him, his still-erect cock in the foreground, I could tell we weren't done. He was still half animal.

I was getting better at knowing which man I was looking at.

He stripped me down and we began in earnest.

Chapter Sixteen

CADEN

Blackthorne Solutions.

The dark room was about six feet by six feet and painted black. I sat in a chair in the center, a clicker in each hand, keeping my eyes on the dot of light on the wall in front of me. To the right and left, in my peripheral vision, photos were projected in pairs at a faster and faster pace.

RIGHT: A child in a pirate costume.
LEFT: A child with a black eye.
(click left)

I answered as I was told, choosing the more violent image without forethought. The Thing didn't have a say. But it wanted one. It had opinions, and I had to think around it before I clicked.

RIGHT: Viet Cong shooting a man in the head.

LEFT: A flower with drooping petals.
(click right)

It was always there now, starting as a whisper in the shadows and growing into a scream in the darkness every day, every hour, every breath.

RIGHT: A dead fish on the shore.
LEFT: A dog with cigarette burns in its eyes.
(click left)

I was coping. I changed my methods as often as I could think of a new way to drive it away. Running out of ideas wasn't an option, and Ronin's call had come just in time.

RIGHT: The blood and guts of surgery.
LEFT: A butcher cutting a side of beef.
(click right)

The lights went on. I took the electrodes off my head. A young tech came in from the back and helped me with the wrist monitors. She was Korean without a trace of an accent. Her name was Mimi, and it belied her seriousness.

"Did I pass?" I asked.

"There's no pass or fail," she said.

I knew that. They kept saying it as if it was true.

I looked to the right, where a small one-way window hid the camera. "Ronin, did I pass?"

His voice came over the speakers. "I'll meet you in the hall."

BLACKTHORNE SOLUTIONS COULD MEAN ANYTHING. The corporate name was so generic, and its parent company's holdings so broad, you could research your heart out and never find out what was going on. But the offices took up three high floors in an expensive office building overlooking the East River.

Ronin met me by reception, dressed in jeans and a crisp white shirt. He led me to a stairway he accessed with a thumbprint. "Hope you don't mind walking up two flights."

"I think I'll make it."

I hadn't spent long in the military compared to Ronin and Greyson, but I'd been there long enough to know I was considered some kind of indolent ass for not enduring basic training.

He had to use his fingerprint to get onto the next floor, and my retinas had to be scanned to get into the back offices. Everything was white and dark gray wood, glass, and chrome. Ronin walked slightly ahead, saying nothing until we arrived in his corner office and he closed the door.

He took a folder off the desk and sat on a tweed couch, indicating I should sit in the love seat opposite him. "Do you want anything? Coffee? Tea?"

I wanted coffee, but it was late in the day. I wanted him to just get to whatever was in that folder. "Water's fine."

He nodded but didn't get up or call for anything. "So here's the deal. You heard a little about what we do here."

"You invent new ways to kill people."

"We like to call it defense development."

"How slippery."

"You expected any less?" He looked up as if alerted. "Come in."

There had been no knock, but the door behind me clicked open. A man in his early twenties brought in a tray with a coffee carafe, two cups, a bottle of water, and a glass of ice. He set them on the table between us, poured, and left without a word.

"That's a neat trick." I looped my finger in the cup's handle. If he'd gone to the trouble of reading my mind, I might as well acknowledge it by having the coffee.

"Not really." He dumped cream into his and drank.

"Greyson says you guys dated."

"We met in basic." He shrugged. "We were nineteen."

"She was eighteen," I corrected. He should have this shit down cold. "Do you have any feelings about what we told you?"

"I didn't marry her. You did."

"You're not concerned about her on a personal level?"

"Have you met her?" His question came out with a cough of a laugh. "She can handle herself."

"Then why take me on if you're not doing her a favor?"

"I didn't say she wasn't my friend. I'll do her favors, but you're also a good candidate. Believe me, I couldn't do a thing if you weren't right for it."

"Can you tell me what makes me right for it?"

"No. We're under contract with a few government agencies. The program you're looking to enter is paid for by Defense." He put down the cup. "The DoD's real particular about who we test on."

"Liability, right?"

"Right. There are some pretty risky trials running right now. What we're thinking for you isn't on that list, but there are still hoops and a very strict NDA." He pushed the folder toward me and picked up his coffee. "You might want to take it home, but if you leave it in the cab and the *Times* prints it, you could wind up in Leavenworth."

"This isn't Kansas anymore." I opened the folder and skimmed. Hold harmless. Liability release. Federal arbitration in the DC courts. FOIA clause. I wasn't a lawyer, but I'd seen versions of most of it before.

"There's one thing that's not in there because it's a prerequisite."

"What?" I closed the folder.

"You have to be active service."

I tossed the folder on the table. It landed with a slap. "That's out."

"I can probably swing it with you on reserve duty. You're IRR, right?"

"I was on a four-year MSO."

"Crap," Ronin said. "Surgeons get blown when they sign on."

"Not quite."

"You can still sign on for the reserves."

"No." I stood up to leave.

"IRR. Individual Ready Reserve," he said as if I didn't know what IRR stood for. "You stay home. No training. That's the last carrot I have."

"I'm not a root vegetable guy, but thanks."

Having refused the carrot, I left without considering the stick.

I WAS LOSING HER. I knew it happening and I'd stepped right into it.

No one, least of all a psychiatrist, wanted to live with a crazy person. I didn't want to come home to open heart surgery either.

Yet the more I tried to get a handle on it, the worse it got. And the more I let loose and tried to stop worrying, the faster the Thing came back. It was always there now, and the days between breaking her got fewer and fewer. Sometimes we'd be at it on normal days and I'd get rough and demanding anyway. But unless I was on the edge, the Thing couldn't see it.

"Did you do the test with Ronin today?" Greyson asked when she came upstairs from her last session. She'd had to take evening hours to accommodate patients with day jobs.

I held her close and kissed her. She tasted of the handful of almonds she'd wolfed down between patients.

"Yeah," I said.

"What was it?"

"Trigger test. I don't think I pass muster."

"Maybe he's working on something else." She slid away from me.

Her optimism only highlighted the fact that she was losing hope. I couldn't shatter it, nor could I bear to hear her ask me if I wanted to enlist in the reserves. I decided right then that I wouldn't tell her. All her hope would flow there.

"He's working on sending you every vet he comes across."

"I have a hard time telling these guys they can't see me." She got a jug of OJ from the fridge and gave it a hard shake. "You see the hard time we're having getting someone for you."

The fridge clicked on, and I stiffened. I was so sick of hearing a voice in the hum of technology that I got annoyed at the appliances.

"'Getting someone for me.'" I walked the length of the kitchen for no reason. "I'm a patient now. A run-of-the-mill nutcase with scheduling issues."

"Caden." She poured juice into a glass. "Don't do this."

"Do what? I'm the guy with a paranoid delusion that something's watching me."

Juice in hand, she came close to me, and I didn't want her to. Not unless she wanted my dick in her ass.

It had been five days.

She didn't take this seriously. She thought I was a case to be cured. I hadn't told her everything because I didn't want to scare her, but maybe that was the problem. She was coming at me, sliding her hand under my jacket, and with her big eyes and her perfume, it was risky. I was dangerous and she was pushing and pushing in ways she couldn't understand.

Her perfume wasn't soothing anymore. It boiled every emotion together. I didn't even know which one I was reacting to anymore.

"Did I tell you this Thing wants to fuck you?"

She stopped the glass halfway to her lips.

I continued. "It's obsessed with you. It thinks I don't deserve you."

"Caden." She was level and serious, as if she was going to lay down the law. Speak the truth. Get the true fucking facts. "This is your fear that you don't deserve good things."

"Oh, is it?"

"This is you punishing yourself."

What I'd been holding back herniated, popping past the membrane of resistance fully-formed, blood-red and screaming. My Thing bridged days of suppression, begging for release to be the man she needed.

"Punishing myself for what?" I stepped toward her.

She didn't budge. She wouldn't. I knew her that well.

"You were overworked."

Fallujah again. The rows of bodies and the fast decisions.

"I was doing my job. For the hundredth time—"

"You're driving me away because you think you don't deserve to be happy."

"You think I'm making this up because I have *guilt*?"

"I never said you were making it up. Your experience is real, but denying this is a defense mechanism isn't helping you."

She was minimizing it, but she wasn't. She saw clearly where I didn't. She was honest and loyal. She was brave. Very brave.

Because she knew there was a battle in my soul, yet she still stirred it.

"Greyson." I put my hand on her throat and slid it back to the base of her silken hair. Her lips loosened and she blinked quickly. Her nipples would be hard, and she'd be most of the way to wet. I could take her right there. I could fuck the courage and honesty right out of her. "You're a warrior. I don't deserve you, but not for the reasons you think."

I released her and walked to the front of the house. I needed air. I needed space. I needed to avoid turning my rawness against her.

A force hit me from behind, slamming me against the couch. I bent over the arm and righted myself, turning toward her. She was red-faced, hair webbed over her eyes, teeth bared, hands up and ready to strike.

"Let it out. Just let it go," she growled, pushing me again.

She could hit much harder. For all her bravado, she was holding back.

That insight came from a cold place, and the cold place was colder than ever while the warm place where the Thing lived ran hotter.

And there we were.

Half a step toward her, and she didn't move.

"You think I'm crazy?" I said.

"I never said that."

"I'm not the crazy one." Another step. She took half a step away, then shoved my shoulder. "You're the crazy one."

"Stop running away. Face it, Caden. Face me."

She vibrated with frustration, rippling like a flag in a hurricane. She raised her fist to hit my shoulder again, but I grabbed her wrist before it hit home.

She wanted me to face her? She was getting faced.

I twisted her arm behind her back and threw her over the couch, holding her wrist against the small of her back. She looked back at me with utter defiance, daring me to finish or not. I put my hand on her cheek and pushed her head into the cushions.

Leaning over, I spoke firmly into her ear. "This is me facing you."

I let her face go and pulled down her pants. Her eggshell ass glowed in the lamplight. Eye to eye, she watched over her shoulder as I pulled my cock out of my pants.

"Tell me if it hurts and let's see if I give a shit."

Without preamble or a courtesy stretch, I shoved inside her as far as I could. I was balls deep in two thrusts and she bit back a scream, writhing. I yanked her arm back and grabbed her hair, fucking her through her cries. With every slap of my body against her ass, the whirlwind intensified. The thick, hot liquid of the unknown force watching me, and the brittle ice of who I was spun in a blinding cone of light and dark.

When I came, all the air left my body. My heat entered her and I was awake again.

"Please," she wept. "Let go."

She was really crying, and I had her right wrist twisted behind her back.

"Shit." I let go and lifted her.

Inside the sound of my wife's sobs, where wet hitch met breathy exhale, where true guilt met broken sorrow, the Thing spoke. For the third time, the whisper between whispers made verbal sense.

It had a name.

Damon.

Chapter Seventeen

Caden was a star, so the Mt. Sinai ER took me right through triage. They gave me painkillers, took a scan, and put my arm in a sling. It wasn't broken, but the nerve damage I'd sustained in basic training had been aggravated. Twenty minutes ice. Twenty of heat. Ice. Heat. Ice. Heat.

It was almost midnight when we drove back from the hospital in silence. He'd wanted to tell them in fine detail how my wrist got fucked up, but I jumped in and told them I tripped on the edge of the rug and fell on it.

He tried to carry me up the stairs.

"I hurt my wrist, not my ankle."

"*I* hurt your wrist, Greyson. I don't care what you told them."

"I can walk."

At the door, he stopped before opening it. "I don't want to go in the house and act like this is normal."

"We won't."

He opened the door. We took off our coats and shoes. Observing a reverent silence, he helped me with both. I went into the kitchen before he could signal where he wanted to go. He wasn't doing this shit. Not on my time. No gently laying me on the couch or tucking me into bed. If we came at this as if he had something to make up for, we weren't going to get anywhere.

"Are you hungry?" he asked.

"I want to set something straight," I said.

"Okay." His pride was held together with spit and chewing gum.

"You're not yourself."

"That's not an excuse."

"It's not. But it's also part of the equation. Whatever's going on, it's not going to be fixed today, tomorrow, next week... maybe ever. So we either go through this cycle over and over, or we get control of it."

"Or we break up."

"Not an option."

"You're really going to take this as far as you can, aren't you?" he said with a rueful smile, challenging me. I didn't know how to walk away from a challenge.

"They don't call me Major One More for nothing."

I took the gel pack off my arm. It had gone lukewarm. I flung it into the microwave and powered it up.

"Has it occurred to you that I can really hurt you? I wanted to choke you."

"Was it erotic asphyxiation, or did you really want to kill me?"

"You're pretty blithe about it."

"Did you want to engage in risky but pleasurable actions, or did you want to commit murder but stopped?"

"The former, but that's not the point."

"What's the point then? Even when you're deep in it, you don't want to hurt me any more than is enjoyable. You're a doctor. You'll know when to stop."

"That's a shitty rationalization. You're better than that."

He rubbed his eyes for longer than a person usually rubs away tiredness. I pulled his arms down. He looked beaten.

"What do you have, Greyson? Because I have nothing."

"And Ronin's treatment isn't going to work?"

"No."

"Did he say that?"

"In so many words."

"When Ronin asked—"

"Fuck Ronin."

I tucked my free hand into his. I couldn't let disappointment grip me. It was too easy to lapse into depression over ungranted wishes. "He asked if it was a pain thing or a control thing."

"And?"

"And you never answered him."

"I don't know. Both maybe. It's hard to get a handle on it right after. Give me... at this rate, twelve hours."

The microwave dinged. He got up and popped it open before I had a chance to assert myself. Flipping the gel pad from one hand to the other while saying *hot-hot-hot*, he reminded me of a carnival juggler, starting low and getting more daring. He flipped it, spun it, tossed it from one hand to the other before whirling it like pizza dough until I laughed.

He lobbed it high, pulled the dish towel off the rack, and caught it with his hand protected by the fabric. I put my wrist on the counter, and he put the warm pad over it, keeping it steady with a firm hand.

"Ah, that's nice," I said.

"Good."

"I was thinking."

"Uh-oh."

"About what Ronin asked, and don't say—"

"Fuck Ronin."

We smiled together, and he kissed me.

"Would you be less afraid of hurting me if we tried to focus more on giving you control?"

He looked at my arm, his mouth twisted with consideration, as if he was holding his thoughts back.

"Well?" I asked.

"We could try it. But I'm warning you." He put an upraised finger between us. "You'd better be controllable, or we're going back to pain."

"Promise?"

"Promise."

He put his free arm over my shoulder and held me. I buried my face in his chest. I could hear his heart beating, red, warm, alive, and vital, home in its cage.

WITH MY ARM IN A SLING, I had to completely cancel two days' worth of sessions and truncate a full week to only the most needy patients. The painkillers made it hard to think quickly enough to engage properly, and the orthopedist had recommended a week of elevation and rigidity, which I couldn't deliver. Two days would have to do.

I spent the time finishing up my proposal for the Gibson Center. A state-of-the-art mental health facility for post-war trauma. Synergy with VA hospitals in three states. Transportation. Outreach and medication stability for homeless vets. A licensed day care center for children while their parents were in counseling or treatment.

I put ten weeks' of research into fifty pages of narrative and a general operating budget that took two weeks to write. I'd listened to the trials of the vets in my office and tried to find solutions. It was the best thing I'd ever done.

Five days after Caden brought me home from the ER, the sling was an optional annoyance and the proposal was ready. I emailed Tina.

DEAR DIRECTOR MOLINO,

I'VE FINISHED THE PROPOSAL. Thank you so much for the extension.

I am on reduced hours for the next two weeks, so I'll be free to preview it for you ahead of the board of directors meeting.

I look forward to showing you the project.

DR. GREYSON FRAZIER, M.D.

I TIDIED the waiting room one-handed. The pain in my wrist had gone from a dull throb to a sharp tremor that ran to my shoulder. The nerve had been damaged when I broke it in basic training. As much as my marriage to Caden was the result of the horrors of war, the best parts of my life were the result of falling on my wrist in my first week as a soldier.

The army had always been my goal. My father and older brother, Jake, were in the army. Both had commissions and careers that contained adventure and excitement inside an orderly routine. Only Colin had no interest in serving, and Mom still gave him a hard time about it. Meanwhile, she had been surprised when I signed up. She juggled surprise, pride, and an inability to understand my motivations. That was understandable, since I didn't really understand them either. Not fully.

I was going to be a medic. There was no war at the time, but that didn't stop me from fantasizing about scrambling through muddy trenches with my kit, telling wounded men they'd be all right, patching them up to be moved under enemy fire. I would be their rescuing angel.

Then I smashed my wrist in basic training. I couldn't put weight on it. Couldn't hold anything too heavy for too long. There was no way I could manage the physical demands of a combat medic. Nor could I hold a rifle for a long time, nor squeeze a trigger repeatedly. War or no war, I couldn't train for jobs I'd never be ready to do.

"You can get an honorable discharge," the army therapist had said.

He was in his sixties, and I'd never forget his name. Dr. Matt

Darling. I'd been sent to him to see if I wanted to be counseled out.

"I'm not quitting." At eighteen, I was stubborn with a side of petulance.

"But you resist the assignments you're qualified to do."

"I don't want to push paper. I want to help people. This is what I'm here for."

He looked over my file. "You applied for combat medic training."

"Yes."

He closed the folder. "Have you considered nursing school? You can stay in the service while you finish." He shrugged. "The army pays. You'd be helping people."

Nursing school. Sure. I could do that. My mother had suggested it too, and at the time, I'd been irritated with her for thinking small.

"Why not med school?" I retorted.

My answer should have slapped back at Dr. Darling the same way it had her. But it didn't.

"Why not?"

I was surprised he didn't laugh at me. He folded his hands in front of him and asked me to decide what was possible and what wasn't. No adult had ever given me that power.

"Why did you become a psychiatrist?" I asked.

"Because it's easy to fix the body. The mind though? Once that's broken, it's hard to set right again, but if you do help someone set it back, they can overcome anything."

I'd thought about that for a long time. Studying for my MCATs, applying to schools and Armed Forces medical scholarships, I thought about helping soldiers like my dad and brother. Somehow, that first desire had landed me at this desk, with my own practice and a husband I loved more than life itself.

After laying the magazines in a row, dusting the shelves, and watering the plants, I checked my email.

DEAR DR. GREYSON,

Congratulations on finishing. I'm excited to see the results.

Let's schedule a time to preview the proposal before the board meeting.

~Tina

I GAVE her a date range and let my hands rest on the desk. I thanked God for the opportunity to make a difference. Success or failure, the attempt was a blessing.

My phone rang. I flipped it open. "Hello?"

"Greyson." It was Caden, and his voice was shiny, hard stone.

So soon. Every time the days between his needs became manifest shortened, I was surprised.

"Tonight," he continued. "Now."

"The control thing?"

The flatness became derisive. "The control thing."

Pain or control? Some combination of both? We'd gone over the possibilities in fine detail, set ground rules, and waited for the presence of the Thing he now called Damon to become unbearable.

He had no Damon in his past. When he was at work, I'd gone through the list of casualties in Fallujah. No Damon. The name was a mystery to me, but personality bifurcation was a mystery to everyone. It had no real rules.

"Now?" The stack of papers bent in my fingers. I loosened my grip on them and laid the stack flat.

"Where are you?"

"In my office."

"Get undressed."

I paused. We'd imagined this differently, but we'd also known to expect the unexpected.

I unbuttoned my blouse and pulled it down my arm, careful of the twinge in my right wrist.

"Tell me what you're doing."

"I was getting ready to double-check the propo—"

"With your clothes."

"Unhooking my bra." I wiggled out of it around the phone. "Now I'm pulling my pants down."

Did I sound irritated? I shouldn't. I should be pliant and submissive regardless of my mood at the moment. That was the deal.

"Leave them around your ankles."

"It's done." Between my desk and the chair, I stood half undressed, waiting. On his side, I heard a whoosh of sudden street noise and the slap of a car door closing. "Caden?"

"I'm coming to the office door."

One step toward it and the pants restricted me. "Can you get in? Do you have the key?"

"Get on your knees."

Through the layers of distraction and annoyance, the command was enough to send a shudder up my spine. That was what I was looking for. There was a name for someone who sexualized the enjoyment of pain. It was masochist. There was also a name for someone who became aroused when obeying commands. It was "sexual submissive." I was that as well.

I got on my knees.

He must have heard my breath change when I got down, because he spoke. "Good girl."

I didn't need his affirmation, Goddammit. This was humiliating enough.

A minute ago, I'd been elated over finishing the proposal, and I was a willing participant in this process. But I didn't have a switch I could flip up or down. I had a dial with a thousand settings that sometimes moved and sometimes didn't.

Right now, it wasn't turned far enough to enjoy this.

"On your elbows."

"I can't... the phone."

"Put the phone in your teeth."

I knew his voice. I knew his levels of detachment and dissociation. He was deep in, and there was only one way out. Through me.

I clamped the thinnest part of the device in my teeth and crawled to the open part of the room so I had space to drop.

Then I thought, *There should be a map.*

Yes! That was an outstanding idea. A map to go with the transportation guidelines. There would be visual learners on the board of directors, and they needed to *see* how far the program could reach.

Leaning back, I snapped a pencil out of the cup.

"Is it done?" Caden said over the phone.

"Mm-hm," I hummed around the phone as I scrawled MAP on a Post-it and slapped it on the proposal cover. A drop of spit fell from my bottom lip to the blotter. I scurried into the position he'd demanded.

"How does it feel?" he asked.

I was in belly crawl position in my office. It felt as though I was dropping to run an obstacle course.

"Ike asic," I said around the phone.

"Yes," he said. "Like basic."

"Oo inoo asic."

"I know I didn't do basic. And you're not supposed to argue."

"Oh-ay."

I waited.

And waited.

I was drooling around the phone and my ass was getting cold. I wondered if I should get the proposal proofread before I showed it to Tina. I wanted to present my best face, but if she had a ton of changes, a proofread would be a waste of time.

Finally, I heard his footfall on the back stairs, and his black shoes appeared under trouser cuffs. He stopped in the doorway. I looked up at him, and he looked down at me. I became acutely aware of my position and my choice to maintain it.

He took the phone out of my mouth and snapped it closed before placing it on the filing cabinet behind the desk. "You're beautiful like this."

Great. Thanks.

"And it upsets Damon, which I enjoy."

He didn't sound as if he was enjoying anything. He sounded as though he was reporting the weather in the tri-state area. All the more reason to play along. He was sick. He needed me. Without me, he'd descend into this hard, brittle personality.

"Crawl to me," he said.

I put one elbow in front of the other, lowering my pelvis as close to the ground as possible so I could fit under the wire.

Of course, this wasn't basic, but I'd been trained to do things a certain way.

"Stop," he said, coming around me.

I put my head down so he couldn't see my face. He put his hands on either side of my hips and lifted them, then he pressed my lower back down.

"Better." He went back to the doorway. "Now. Crawl."

I moved a knee forward, and my butt dropped. When I moved my other knee, it would drop farther. I was supposed to present myself like a cunt-proud peacock and—

"Honestly, Caden?" I got up on my knees and rested on my haunches. "Not today."

He raised an eyebrow and leaned on the jamb with his arms crossed. Not offended or hurt, which was good, but he'd locked away his emotions so tight, he *couldn't* feel insulted. That was not good.

"I just finished the proposal for the hospital's PTSD unit."

"Yes?"

"How about... you know, congratulations?"

"You can't tell me this later?"

I got up. "I'm telling you now." I pulled up my pants and fastened them. "You could play along for fifteen minutes before dropping this on me."

"So could you."

I swung my blouse over my shoulders. "Sure. I could. I could. And I agreed to. But I just can't crawl around right now. I want to feel happy. I want to feel proud, and I want to be excited for my meeting."

I got to the top button and realized I'd forgotten my bra. Damnit. I didn't want to take the shirt off again. I wanted to finish getting dressed. I wanted to tell him all the things in the packet. I wanted his feedback and his joy, not this. Not today.

"You know what I want?" I said. "A celebratory fuck."

"I can't deliver that right now. Not in a way you'd find honest."

"And I can't let you control me right now. Not in a way I'd find honest."

Not waiting for his reaction, I left the office and went upstairs.

Living room and kitchen. Didn't want to eat. Didn't want to sit. I wanted to think about something besides my husband's mental health, or anyone else's for that matter. But he was at the bottom of the stairs, a pressure from below, squeezing me into a corner.

Footfall on the steps. A creak. Slowly, as if he wasn't sure he should come or as if creeping up on me.

I couldn't deal with his stone-cold face. It wasn't him. This was a single dimension of the multi-dimensional human I loved. Neither one of us had control over this situation. I couldn't be mad at Caden any more than I could be mad at a bird for shitting on my shoulder.

"Greyson?" he called from the stairs, raising his voice only enough to make sure I heard, as if he had a complete understanding of the physics of space and sound and used it to make sure I knew he was still in control.

The tone was hard to ignore. The command was so complete, I thought maybe if I went to the top of the stairs and kneeled, we could continue with the game and he'd be pleased. Damon would run. I'd have so many orgasms, I'd pass out in a heap. We could be normal inside of three hours.

Wanting one thing meant not wanting another, no matter how agreeable I made it sound to myself. I went to the foyer and plucked my coat off the hook.

"Greyson?" he called louder as he came up the stairs. I was punching my hands into my coat sleeves when he appeared from the living room. "Where are you going?"

"I don't know. But I can't do this. Not today. And I can't be in this house with you right now."

"I should say I'm sorry now."

"I'll accept that as the best apology you can deliver in this state."

A flicker passed over his face. A lake perfectly reflecting a statue, then rippling. Was it regret? A rethinking of his assumptions? A change in strategy? All of them?

"I keep thinking about you first," I said. "I keep asking myself what you need, and I'm happy to give it to you. I love you. But today? It's about me and what I need. You can't give it to me. Fine. I get it. But I have nothing to give right now."

I opened the front door, and he came for me, grabbing me at my new favorite spot. The hair on the back of my head. I gasped.

"When are you coming back?"

"Stop."

The flicker again. The ripple in the cold lake. My Caden was in there.

He let me go, dropping his hand completely. His body was still. No nervous tics. No tells for displeasure or discomfort.

I'd married a fucking robot.

"I'll come back when I do."

I walked out, closing the door behind me.

I breathed the outside air, exhaled a wintry cloud, and went down the steps onto 87th Street with no destination except relief.

COLIN MET ME FOR A MOVIE. It was loud and fast. The sensory overload pushed my sadness and anxiety into a corner but didn't eradicate it.

"Wasn't that better than the depressing French thing?" Colin asked outside the theater as he wrapped his scarf around his neck.

"Sure."

"So," he said, hands in his pockets, looking up the street for a free cab. "What's going on with the man of the house?"

"How do you mean?"

"You called me for a spur-of-the-moment movie. You don't do that. If I want to see you, I have to make plans a month in advance."

I bounced on the balls of my feet, trying to find the happiness I'd earned. "The proposal I told you about? For Mt. Sinai? I finished it."

"All right! Congratulations! Are we getting a drink?"

A drink was so much more appealing than dealing with Doctor Robot.

THE LIGHTING WAS minimal and the patrons were all in the hippest years of their twenties. Colin had unbuttoned his coat, exposing his neck. The bartender, a young woman with the flattest, smoothest stomach I'd seen on anyone since treating Iraqi refugees, couldn't keep her eyes off it. I held my credit card out for her, but my brother pushed my hand away and held out his card. The bartender pursed her lips and eyed his hand, then his face, holding back a smile.

"Oh, for Chrissakes." My grumble was drowned out by the music.

When she took his card, she touched his hand.

"I could be your girlfriend, you know," I said.

"You used a card to buy the last round. Same name." He brought his drink to his smiling lips.

"I could be your wife."

He waved his bare left ring finger at me with a devilish wink.

"Remember when I had to be your prom date?" I asked. "You asked three girls and they all said yes?"

"You were a fun date."

"And you made out with all three of them anyway."

"You were dancing with... what's his name?"

"I had one foot in a recruitment office, so I was dancing with everyone."

"Thanks for taking one for the team." Colin still thought my entry into the military had spared him the pressure to do the same. I wasn't sure Dad wasn't aware Colin wasn't cut out to be bossed around all day. "Mom hasn't seen you since you came back."

I sipped my drink. Not bad. They didn't have wine, so I'd ended up with a whiskey and mint concoction, and Colin had gotten something with a vanilla bean sticking out of it. The bartender dropped the check in front of us with his card on top.

"I'm waiting for Dad to get back. She knows that."

Dad was in Japan, and Mom was doing what she did—wait for him to come back. It was the gender-reversed version of the life I'd avoided by retiring with Caden.

"Well, she's not telling you, but she's talking about coming here." He signed the receipt before showing me that his copy had her number on it.

"Jake was in North Carolina for how long before he saw them? Was she chewing off your ear then?"

"You're the baby girl. You weren't supposed to be in the military at all."

"I wasn't supposed to have my own life at all."

"And she's wound up about you guys being in Medical Corps. From what Dad says, the surge is still going and they're deploying doctors and nurses whether they like it or not. He said you guys dodged a bullet leaving when you did. Anyone with a medical license and a pair of boots is getting stop-lossed."

"I'm not going back. Neither is Caden. We're both done." I slapped my hands together to illustrate the done-ness of our service obligations.

"Are you all right?"

"Yeah. Why?"

"You loved the army. I thought you wouldn't be able to adjust to having your own life."

I couldn't tell him that my life wasn't my own or who it belonged to. I knew what the warning signs of abuse were, which was why I'd lied to the hospital staff about my wrist. Isolating the victim. Mercurial personality changes. Sexual demands. A rising tide of injuries.

No one would understand what was going on in my house, especially not my little brother.

"It's hard," I said. "I'm used to knowing what I'm doing every day and having this huge support system."

"That fails constantly?"

"At least when the pipes broke on base, Mom knew who to call. I don't know where the boundaries are out here."

"Is something going on I should know about?"

"No. Everything's fine. But like with the bartender here? Of course she saw the names, but I promise you she was eyefucking you before you handed her your card. And that's not even the thing. Sure, it happens in the service, but it doesn't feel so strange because I understand the context. Multiply that by a billion little things."

Colin finished his drink and pushed the glass to the back edge of the bar. "Sister, dear, you are the most competent person I know. That's the only reason you're doubting your competence. We doubt what we're gifted with."

"And what do you doubt?"

He smirked. "I doubt you could walk a straight line. You're swaying like a boat. Should I get you a cab?"

I finished my drink and plopped it on the bar, flicking two fingers against the bottom to slide it over to Colin's. They clinked together. "Let's blow this shithole."

"We have to talk about Mom," he said when we were outside. "If she comes, she's staying with you."

With me? Where Caden did violent, painful, intense things to my body?

I agreed to talk about it, but no more.

THE HOUSE WAS empty and quiet. Caden's coat was gone. A note sat on the counter.

Major -
I got a call. I'll be at the hospital. Come by the theater some time
if you feel like watching.
- Captain

Short, businesslike, to the point.

"Roger," I said with a little slur on the edges, tossing the note on the counter.

Fine. It was fine. I needed to get to sleep anyway. I could worry about my husband tomorrow. I trudged up the stairs, hanging on to the banister. Colin had been right. I couldn't walk a straight line to save my life.

The empty bed was made; an accusatory rectangle with military corners and sheets so tight a quarter would bounce twice on it.

You failed him.

Having let in the first thought I'd been avoiding, the next ones came without being invited.

He needed you and you failed him.

You're the healthy one. You need to step up.

I stripped down, leaving my clothes on the floor, and put on a big army T-shirt.

You enjoy it anyway.

You need to just let go.

"I do enjoy it," I grumbled, getting off the toilet. "But not today. Not today."

I saw myself in the bathroom mirror.

"You," I said with all the authority the whiskey-and-mint drink let me muster, "you are awesome. You did a great job."

I opened the medicine cabinet, retrieved the toothbrush and toothpaste, and snapped it closed to see my face again. "No. Really. No arguments."

I squeezed toothpaste on my brush and got to work. Despite my mouth being occupied with daily hygiene, the woman in the mirror wasn't finished talking.

"Ou can 'ake a 'ight 'or-ooself. Ou did-a'ight 'hing. 'Oor no 'ood 'oo him 'essed uhp."

The woman in the mirror was right. I was useless to Caden if my resources were depleted. We'd worked out sexual boundaries and needs, but we hadn't talked about the toll his condition, or whatever it was, was taking on me.

I spit the toothpaste.

I could call the shots too. The man I'd married was going to have to live with that. The man he became in the weeks—no, days—between demanding, painful, orgasmic, boundary-pushing sex was going to have to live with it too.

Chapter Eighteen

CADEN

The lubricated slope that slid into the pit of cool detachment got wider and easier to find. I felt relief sliding down it and worried about how easy it was. Was I making a choice anymore, or was I like an addict telling myself the story of a decision I never made?

I didn't leave her alone out of consideration but practicality. Considering her earlier refusal, I wasn't sad or guilty. I couldn't register her needs as important outside my own because Damon was shouting in the desperate corners of my perception. But I knew they existed and I knew what they were. I knew feelings inside me would return and that I'd be glad they were there. Maintaining complete detachment wasn't hard, yet the consequences were exhausting.

It got worse every time.

I didn't wonder if I loved her; I wondered what love was at all.

It was getting harder to pull back.

I had control over what I did to her, but without love to set boundaries or guilt to govern my impulses, when would I start to ask myself what I could get away with?

Without the wherewithal to feel fear, I had to ask myself if I should be afraid.

By the time I left the OR in the morning, one thing had become very clear.

The absolutes were unsustainable.

Not my pattern of madness or her constant patience.

Not my unquestionable demands or her total acquiescence.

The calculation was made to my own detriment, but even in the hardest part of my heart, where the long-term decision happened, the truth of it was the single constant.

This had to end.

EARLY MORNING ON SEPTEMBER 13TH, 2001, I stopped working and started looking for my parents.

At one point, I realized they were never coming back from their morning appointment with their financial advisor. Dad hadn't been with the first responders doing triage or patching the immediately patchable. He hadn't made it to a hospital to offer or receive services. My mother wasn't in a recovery room or wandering around with amnesia.

The flyer I stapled to poles and subway walls had a recent photo of them at a hospital fundraiser. Mom was smiling. When I'd offered to take her away from Dad, she laughed at me. She loved him. She'd never leave him.

I loved him too. I didn't want to love him. He deserved to be despised, but I couldn't. I was a surgeon. And an adult. But all I wanted was to earn his approval.

It was a week before I could stomach the September eleventh videos, and that was when the narrative formed. The jumpers were falling like dried buds off an old Valentine's bouquet, dropping petals of shredded fabric, too fast to identify. Too blurred.

There was a couple holding hands on the way down. They could have been strangers. Friends. Lovers. Married. We'd never know.

The acceleration of gravity is 9.81 seconds per second. They fell for six to eight seconds, depending on wind shear, hitting a velocity of 132 miles per hour. They must have been conscious in freefall. Capable of thought and fear. Capable of peace. Capable of making a decision.

The couple holding hands wasn't Mom and Dad, because I decided that in the end, my mother would have come to peace and realized she was better than the way he treated her.

And Dad? Was he sorry?

Between the place where I trusted Mom had rejected him and

the place where I loved my father enough to wish atonement for him, I hoped he'd died proud of me.

Which was pathetic.

I didn't find peace. I found impotence and rage. On October first, after hanging on to hope for three weeks, I signed up for the war to keep as many soldiers as possible from dying for my father, and to avenge my mother, who never got to avenge her years of abuse.

We weren't anything like Greyson's family. We didn't have a history of military service. My great-grandfather served as an army doctor in World War II and Korea. That was the extent of it.

The country was doing something. We were taking out the bases where the men who'd killed my parents trained. Even if it was too late, it was something. I wouldn't watch vengeance on television.

If I'd had a sense of duty before, it had been hidden. My girlfriend at the time was shocked. She'd thought I was crazy. Rich surgeons didn't sign up for the military. That was for white trash and brown people.

Needless to say, that relationship went down in a sputtering flame from a hundred and ten stories above.

I never looked back.

IN THE DARK LIVING ROOM, with the streetlights casting edges in blue, I waited for Greyson to come home. We had much to discuss.

The tricky part was explaining things to her as the man she'd married, not the monster I was.

I knew my face was somehow different to her when I was like this.

So I unscrewed the bulb from the front hall.

I knew my voice sounded different, because I could hear the hardness as well as she could.

So I wouldn't speak.

Damon swirled desperately in the shadows, so real I was sure I could touch him, but I didn't move. Not when she came up the stoop, carrying a binder, or when she opened the door. Not when she flicked the light for nothing or when she pulled off her coat and dropped her stuff on the chair to try the light again.

I stood.

When she turned and saw my silhouette, she jumped like a colt, then smiled when she realized it was me. "The light's busted."

I took her hand and put it over my lips. She let it linger there, and I slid my mouth to the inside of her wrist and kissed the soft flesh, letting my lips linger over the throb of her pulse.

"You're not mad," she said.

I shook my head to say no and ran my tongue over the inside of her arm, pushing away the sleeve of her blue dress.

"Good. We should talk."

"You talk." The words left my mouth like frozen stones. I wanted control, but I'd spent too much time talking. Too many words gave her space to hear the voice of a man disentangled from his love.

"I'm not sorry about last night," she said. "I wish I could be there for you every time, but sometimes I just can't."

"Mm-hm." I nodded into her skin. My lips ran up her arm to her shoulder, her neck, kissing the curve of her jaw. A wet sigh drifted from her, and her body lost its rigidity.

"Caden," she whispered.

She reached behind her and unzipped her dress. I pushed the neckline apart, over her shoulders. It fell into a puddle of fabric at her feet. The swell of her breasts in the lace bra, the curve of her belly over the panties. The shadow where her thighs met.

"Take it," she said. "Show me what you need."

She'd understood me and, in doing so, made the first crack in the crust I'd put around my emotions. I was hard. Raging. All the plans I'd drawn up while I waited for her were wiped away to be replaced with harder, more precisely cruel ones.

I tapped her lower lip with my index finger and she opened her mouth. I put two fingers along her tongue to the back, pushing against her barrier until she opened her throat. She bent under the pressure, and Damon hissed.

That was it. I had it. I had her.

I spun her and grabbed her from behind, pressing my erection against her. I hooked my finger in her underwear and snapped it. She got them down to her knees with me still holding her against me, and I wedged my hand between her legs. Throbbing and wet. The temptation to get her off quickly and feel that first bite of satisfaction was in the muscles of my hand.

But the other hand wanted more. The other hand wanted to bring her to the edge of death and back again. Collar her with my body. Restrain her most basic bodily function.

My hand on her throat, I tightened just a little.

"Caden." She put her hand over mine. I didn't whisper or speak. I didn't move either hand. I just held her against me, waiting. "Breath play. You want breath play?"

I'd heard of it when a kid in my class hanged himself jerking off, but we called it something different. She was a psychiatrist with hundreds of patients telling her their deepest, darkest secrets. I couldn't do anything she hadn't heard in session. I nodded into her neck.

I waited. I could stand a "no." There were plenty of ways to control her, myself, and the act, but owning her life for even a second was the ultimate, and my cruelest self craved it almost as much as I craved her pain.

There had been something to Ronin's observation, but maybe it wasn't either/or. Maybe I needed both.

She put her weight backward, arching her neck. I felt her swallow against my palm, felt her body take in breath and release it. She didn't answer, and still, I waited.

Finally, she spoke. "I trust you."

I rubbed her clit mercilessly and gently tightened my grip on her larynx.

She jerked. I tightened and rubbed, keeping her still by those two points and the pivot of our hips. As I held her tight, she fought, grabbing my wrist, twisting away. Strong as a soldier, she flung herself away, but still I held her by the clit and the throat.

She pulled my arm. She was scared. That wasn't what I wanted. She needed to trust me.

"*Shh,*" I whispered because it didn't engage the ice in my voice. "*Shh.*"

With a short nod, she stopped resisting. That wouldn't last. Not as I kept her windpipe closed until her face was bulging red. Her body writhed. My hand taking her clit over and over as the physical reaction resumed. She kicked and twisted, knocking over the end table.

Then some of the fight went out of her. I didn't let up the pressure on her nub, but I let go of her throat. She went stiff, coming with a cry and a jolt. Her sucking breath turned into an orgasmic cry. Limbs limp against me, she came and came, toes pointing, hips jerking, spine rigid, eyes rolled to the back of her head.

We bent over the back of the couch, my body curved to hers. We breathed together.

Fuck. I did that. I'd held her life in my hands. Cathartic to say the least.

"Is he gone?" she asked.

"Mostly. Are you all right?"

"Yes. That was..." She closed her eyes and rested her cheek on my arm. "The most intense orgasm I've ever had."

I knew I could speak when guilt wound its way into my heart. I pulled back a little, steadying her on the sofa. My stomach was wet.

"Shit," I said. "I came."

She smiled. "Was it good for you?"

I laughed, or more accurately, the part of me that wasn't capable of laughing allowed the capable part to laugh because it would soothe her. The time between changes was the most uncomfortable, and it drove my unquenchable thirst for her.

"We're not done."

MY FINGERS IN HER CUNT, I had her upper arms tied to the top of the headboard with clamps and latex tubing, leaving her ass six inches from the sheets. She had to use her feet to take the pressure off her arms, and the discomfort she endured for me made me want to see her racked with orgasms. She was close to her fourth of the evening. Her eyes were drooping. Her body jerked when I removed my fingers and put them in her mouth.

"Suck yourself off."

She did it. There was no lipstick left. All the mascara had slid down her cheeks in blue rivulets. She sucked weakly. This would have to be her last one.

Good. I was almost free of the lockdown. Then I'd let the guilt walk right through me, hand in hand with the fear that I'd hurt her or worse.

Wedging my hips under her, I pushed inside her, getting my saliva-slick hand under her chin. "You want to come?"

"Yes." Her throat was shredded from my cock.

"How bad?"

"Bad. Please, I want to come so bad."

Thumbing her clit, I fucked her, timing it so we came together.

That last act of control and release opened me up to what I'd done when I was too cold to feel my love. When I was a monster in a man's body.

What had I done?

SHE WAS IN MY ARMS, sleeping. Tomorrow we'd take stock of her bruising. We'd carve new boundaries and make new rules. The mostly sane man she married would be awake and verbal in the morning, and he'd agree she could say no for whatever reason.

Tomorrow, remorse would fill me like a bucket and Damon would reappear louder and stronger, sooner than ever before.

What I'd done was simple.

I'd agreed to a risk to save her from this nightmare.

Drowning in the gray soup of sleep, I knew I'd made the right decision.

Chapter Nineteen

GREYSON

I was woken at four in the morning when a bus with squeaky brakes stopped somewhere on Columbus. I lay still for a few minutes, letting the warmth of the sheets and the sound of Caden's breathing soak into my senses.

All of the familiar aches were present, along with complete sexual satisfaction. I turned onto my side and tucked my hands under my cheek. He looked like himself again. Even with his face slack in sleep, I could tell he was back.

My Caden.

My captain.

We'd get through this.

Something had happened. I didn't know if it was a breakthrough or the first step in a thousand, but something.

Five days since he'd needed to hurt me. If it was more, or even five again, we'd know.

In four days, we'd know if we could change the course of this thing. Maybe stop it in its tracks. Hope fluttered my heart, and I knew I wasn't getting any sleep.

I slipped out of bed, went to the bathroom, and put on a big T-shirt to go downstairs for a glass of water.

Most PTSD treatments involved sensory or mental exposure to the seed trauma. Caden hadn't landed on exactly what he needed to be exposed to, and I'd thought whatever Ronin was working on would let us circumvent the trauma that either didn't exist or that Caden wouldn't admit to.

That was down the shitter obviously, as was any help from Ronin.

But we had this. I was sure of it.

I rinsed out the glass and went through the living room to the staircase. Caden's jacket was piled on the floor. I picked it up by the collar and shook it out. An envelope came out partway.

The army seal was in the corner.

Probably a pension notice or something. I hung up his coat and took the letter to the second floor, where he kept his office. I didn't turn on the light. I knew what was there. Bookshelves with thick medical texts. A glass-topped desk with a computer. A phone. A leather chair in the corner.

I was about to leave the envelope on his desk, where he'd see it, when something I'd noticed before jabbed at me. There was no sending address or stamp.

Why would that be?

If the army had sent him something, it would be via mail, with a canceled stamp and a sealed flap. This flap wasn't sealed. The only way he'd get an open, unmarked envelope from the US Army was if he met with... who? Where?

Why?

I couldn't even imagine.

Prying into my husband's life wasn't a habit, but I wasn't snooping to see if he was cheating on me or spending money he shouldn't. I expected garbage. A fundraising flyer or a mentor request.

My expectations were lies I told myself to cover for the fact that I had no business opening that envelope or sliding out the paper. Leaning into the window to catch the light from the streetlamps, I opened the single page. It stretched like arms folded in anger slowly unbending for an embrace.

I read it once.

Then again, clutching the thin cotton of my shirt. I twisted it as if my heart was in my fist and by God, I was going to wring it dry before it killed me.

"Honey?" He was at the office door in his pajama bottoms, framed in the molding around the opening. Dark behind him. Lit with the barest window light.

He was a god and a saint. He lined my soul, and as I stood there with my shirt twisted in my fist, he was...

I held out the letter.

...the heart I wanted to wring dry.

"Greyson?"

"No," I said, not denying my name but his. His name did not belong on that paper. "This is a mistake."

Caden came into the room with his hand out for the letter, brows knotted with curiosity and concern. He didn't know what it was.

Hope kept the tears at bay. Hope was the only cure for disappointment—if it didn't kill you first. Hope stuck harder and took a piece of you when it was ripped away.

He opened the letter for the briefest moment then folded it again.

"It's a mistake," I said.

"Let me explain."

No. *No-no-no.* Hope ripped away, leaving pieces of itself behind. I was made of spit and tears, but I held on to them. "It's a mistake, Caden!"

"It's not. I mean, it may be, but—"

"It's not?"

Hope was a fish hook, barbed to leave a jagged hole when removed.

"It's just the reserves."

"Just? You *fuck*." I punched his shoulders with both fists. He didn't fall. He needed to fall so hard he'd break time. Then we could go back ten minutes, before I knew. Back a day, before the letter existed. A decade, before the war. "You fucking *fuck*. How could you do this?"

He held up both hands. "Just take it easy."

I snatched the letter from him and tore it up. "I do not accept this." I threw the pieces at him. "I love you. You are my life, you fucking shit." I punched his chest and he did not defend himself. "I break for you. Do you understand? I break every damned day and you do this? Why? You think getting away from me is going to cure you?"

"It's not that." He grabbed my arms before I could punch him again.

"What then?" I tried to yank away, but he wouldn't let me.

"The treatment. The experimental protocol. I need to be in the system or I don't qualify."

I buckled. I couldn't hold myself up. The floor was despair and I needed to melt into it, flatten myself against it like spilled water, spread and evaporate. Only his hands kept me upright, saving me and killing me with equal force.

"It's IRR. I don't have to do anything. They'll keep me off active duty. Please. Listen—"

"You're going to get called. Do you understand, you stupid, stupid man? They're going to call you back."

I tried to get away, but he held me harder. "They're not. Greyson. Listen to me. They're not calling me."

"You're going to get stop-lossed. They're going to deploy you, send you away, and I swear, Caden, you're not a soldier. You're not meant for it. They're going to send you back broken." My anger melted in its own heat, dripping away in thick tears.

That time he'd gone off-base with a medevac. He'd been so brave and strong inside the hospital walls, and it all fell apart on the front lines. He returned covered in blood, unable to function or process what he'd seen. He wasn't the same after that. His arrogance lost its edge after one time on the front lines. What if he was sent out again? How could he so blithely assume he'd survive it? "Why? Why did you do this?"

"I have to. I can't let you keep taking the brunt of my sickness. It's hurting you. *I'm* hurting you. Grey, I'm..." His face tightened as if he held back his own tears. "I'm afraid I'm going to kill you."

He barely got the last word out before breaking. He let my arms go, and I held him. We bent together, falling as if we'd been detonated, limbs wrapped together like a smoking pile of twisted metal beams, weeping for the end of the life we'd tried to live.

Chapter Twenty

GREYSON

I sat on the stone wall on Central Park South and picked the pickles off my sandwich, eating them one by one. They got less and less shockingly sour with every bite.

The sidewalk was packed with the lunch crowd, and more than once, I had to chase someone away from the spot next to me. A jackhammer pounded the street somewhere. No matter what street I was on, there was always a jackhammer going in New York, as if the city had to remind you not to get too comfortable.

Ronin appeared with a cup of coffee, and I moved my bag so he could sit next to me.

"Afternoon, Major One More."

"Afternoon, Lieutenant Shithead."

"I had the feeling this was the kind of conversation I was in for."

"What you did was fucked up."

I watched a gaggle of tourists wrestle with a map. A businesswoman dug in her bag to pay for a knish. Two guys in suits walked as if they were racing somewhere and talking as if they were on the verge of ending poverty.

"I assume you're talking about Caden going into the reserves," he said.

"I can't even look at you."

"He's a grown man."

"He thinks you can keep him from getting called."

"How do you know I can't?"

I let out a derisive laugh. He'd always had a high opinion of his position.

"This war's messy," I said. "It's never going to end. Every week, it's clearer we're in a quagmire. You know it because your company is invested in keeping it going. War ends, money dries up."

"It doesn't work like that."

"Maybe not for you. For the suits on the top floor? For the lobbyists? That's how it works. And now my husband is on the army's radar. If there's pressure to send him back, you'll buckle. Your company will buckle. And if he goes back..." I took a deep breath and finally looked at Ronin. "If he goes back and he doesn't die, he'll be dead anyway. In his mind, he'll be someone else. I'm not ready to lose him. I'm not ready for my mind to die."

"Okay, let's do this." He put his coffee on the seat and pivoted to face me. "I'm going to tell you things you should have seen already."

"Don't try to tell me how much pull you have."

"I don't have the pull to keep your husband safe because he wants it. I have pull because he's valuable. He has the complete table of criteria for this treatment. He's educated, verbal, aware. If we nail this, it's going to treat PTSD on the field in real time."

"So you can send them back out."

"So we can send them back out. Imagine that though? Healthy men. Stable men. Fighting like they're trained to do. It would crack the recruitment problem wide open."

"How do I know he's not going to be the first guy you cure and send out?"

"Because he's not the only one. We have test subjects from all over who are better suited to going back to the front lines."

I sighed and turned back to the street. A plume of smoke wafted up from Sixth Avenue. Jackhammer debris. Was it possible to enjoy living in a city when it pounded your soul into compliance?

"I don't trust you," I said.

"He does."

"He barely knows you."

"Do you know him?"

I snapped back toward him. The years had rubbed away so much of Ronin's handsomeness, leaving behind a face that was a little more than good-looking, a little less than readable. When Caden stuffed his emotions away, he hid behind a mask of stone. Ronin's mask was made of intensity and enthusiasm.

"Maybe not," I said.

"You don't have to trust me, but you should. I've told you more than I'm supposed to."

"I love him, Ronin. He's my life, and seeing him like this... it hurts me more than you can imagine. If I could put myself in his place, I would."

"My guess is seeing you suffer would hurt him just as much."

"I can handle it better."

"Don't sell him short." He stood and leaned down to pick up his cup. "He can handle more than you think." When he was straight again, he saluted with his cup-hand, two fingers to his forehead. "Later, Major."

"Fuck you, Lieutenant."

Chapter Twenty-One

CADEN

The Blackthorne tech was a young Hispanic woman in a white coat, the picture of seriousness and detachment. She flicked the end of the syringe.

"Right arm," she said.

"What are you giving me?" I rolled up my sleeve.

"B vitamins." She gave me the shot with painful precision. I felt as if I was in the army again.

"Ventrogluteal's safer."

"I'll mention it to management." She collected her tray and left.

THEY PUT me in the same black room I tested in, which was comforting in a way. But the slide choices and the clickers were absent. In its place were a comfortable chair, a table with a soft lamp, and a bottle of water.

"Caden?" a voice came over the speaker.

"Good morning, Ronin."

"I just came by to say it's great to have you."

"Thank you."

"Lee reviewed how you do it, right?"

"In-out, in-out. Been doing it my whole life."

"The pacing is important," he said. "And the depth of the breath."

"This isn't meditation, is it?"

"Not quite."

"Because I don't have time for woo-woo bullshit, okay?"

"This is not woo-woo bullshit."

"All right then." I grasped the arms of the chair and the lamp dimmed.

Ronin was replaced by a woman's recorded voice. She repeated the same two syllables over and over.

Soo-hoo.

"This is ridiculous," I grumbled.

Soo-hoo.

"She's like a mating bird."

The speaker clicked on, and another voice came over the cooing woman. "Just try to relax."

Fine.

I would relax.

For Greyson.

I could do this for Greyson twice a week. I'd given up too much to be in that room, and half a self-conscious effort wouldn't reward my sacrifice or hers.

Soo-hoo.

I breathed in at *soo* and out at *hoo*, starting over without holding either inhale or exhale.

Soo-hoo.

The voice faded into the hiss of my breath, folding like a map into my consciousness.

Soo-hoo. Soo-hoo. Soo-hoo.

Something inside me trembled.

AND SHOOK.

AND TRIED to break but couldn't.

ON THE FOURTH SESSION, I came to a terrifying well of despair, but the tape stopped and the light went bright before I touched it.

IT ALWAYS DID.

Chapter Twenty-Two

"Thank you for meeting me," Tina said as she sat down behind the shiny conference table.

Outside, the western sky dimmed into a burning rust color. Dots of headlights crawled along Fifth Avenue, and the green of the park turned gray.

When we shook hands, my sleeve hiked up. Caden had tied me up three days before, and the bruises had just faded down to yellow.

Like a teacher who called on you for the one answer you didn't know, Tina's eyes fell on the discoloration inside my arm, safely an inch below the wrist. She couldn't know the pains he'd taken to make sure he didn't pinch the nerve. Nor could she know the most pleasurable pain didn't come from the ties.

"I had a cancellation, so it worked out," I said, ignoring the question in her eyes.

"The board's pretty interested in this."

"It's hot in here." She took off her jacket. "Do you want some water?"

"I'm good." I opened the folder and handed her a copy of the proposal with my inner wrist facing the table. "I put in your revisions. I think it's ready for the board."

She nodded and scanned the pages. "I think so too."

"HEY." I had my phone pressed to my ear as I walked down an empty stairway. The walls were bright white with black scuffs. I'd waited at the elevator, but I had too much energy. I didn't wait for Caden to greet me. "I just met Tina. She *loved* it. And I mean loved with a capital L and a heart for an O. She wants me to present it to the board and tell her what kind of position I want!"

Full time? Advisory? Did I want to stay in private practice? Any kind of hybrid? The options were overwhelming and thrilling. So many doors had opened, I couldn't count them.

"That's wonderful," he replied.

I slowed my run. He had been his one true self when he'd kissed me good-bye in the morning. But he wasn't now. It was creeping back. No one would notice but me. He sounded so close to normal, maybe a little tired, but he was in the beginning of Damon's cycle.

I stopped on a landing. There was going to be a course correction. "Where are you?"

"In my office. I just got out of the OR."

"What floor is that on?"

"Where are you, Major?"

"Between seven and eight. On the stairs."

"Meet me on six."

I hung up. My heels clattered and echoed off the metal steps and stark walls.

The door to the sixth floor slapped open, and he was there. Clean-shaven for cutting day. Collar open to the edges of the hair on his chest. Thick watch setting the boundary for the precision of his hands. Eyes of cold, dark sapphire that would get darker and colder very soon.

He reached out as I came to the last step and kissed me. Possessed me. Devoured me. I had so much to say, but I was consumed in that kiss.

"It's working," I said when I could breathe. "You're holding."

"I know. I know. We were down to eighteen hours. Now it's three days."

"Three whole days."

He squeezed me so hard I left the floor and only let go enough to kiss me again. "I just want a minute to kiss you like this. Taste you before I get taken over."

I forgot about the sleeves and the bruises. About the meeting with Tina and what she'd offered at the end.

He was in there with me, kissing my mouth and my neck like a starving man. Nothing else mattered. Nothing.

He put hands on both sides of my face and yanked himself away.

"I love you," he said through his teeth as if carving it in his mind.

"Three days."

"Then five. Then a week." I hooked my hands at his elbows and touched his forehead with mine. "I never thought I'd be grateful to Ronin for anything in my life."

"It's changing fast though."

"Tonight then." I couldn't help but smile.

"When this is all over—" He kissed my lips, flicking his tongue inside them. "When I'm normal again, I'm not going to stop."

"Stop what?"

He kissed my face between every act. "Tying you down. Spanking you. Hurting you. Pushing you. Owning you. Marking you."

"Deal." I pushed him away, and his face darkened as if the change was coming in with a tide.

"Be naked when I get home."

"I'LL BE THERE in five minutes," he said over the phone as I paced the living room. "Are you naked?"

"Yes. I'm ready."

"I'm going to destroy you whether you're ready or not."

He hung up.

My plan was to get destroyed, then before he went cold again, we would talk about my options with the hospital and my practice. I couldn't figure out how to manage the time. Many doctors melded the two; I didn't know how. The normal Caden would know what to do. The man who was coming home was a trusted keeper of my body and my orgasms, but my career was off-limits.

Passing the mirror by the front door, I stopped. My hair draped over my shoulders like a veil. I pulled it into a twist and over one shoulder.

Three days.

The time between episodes was getting longer. The crescent of light that glowed when the dark eclipsed the light had gotten slimmer and slimmer. Totality never came. The moon was already moving away from the sun.

There was a knock at the front door, and I froze. Why didn't he come in?

Did he want me to open the door naked onto 87th Street?

The satin lining of my coat was cool on my back. I checked myself in the mirror and let the collar loose so it fell over my shoulders as I clutched the placket together at my breast. I opened the door. Colin stood under the front light.

"Jesus, Colin!"

"You invited me for dinner. Where are you g—?" He stopped himself when he saw my bare feet, then he raised an eyebrow at me, a smile curling one side of his mouth.

"Not tonight."

I tried to close the door in his face, but he held it open. "Are you all right?"

I got the coat up around me. "I double-booked. Sorry. We have to get dinner another time."

"Sis. What's going on?"

"My husband's getting home for the first time after days of back-to-back surgery. I'd like to spend my evening doing what married people do, not letting my brother continually ask what's wrong, okay?"

The gears in his head turned. Behind him, people walked the street below. I was a woman in a coat talking to a man on my stoop.

What I wouldn't have done for a porch and a driveway.

"Fine, I get it. You two. Jesus." He shook his head.

"Tomorrow," I called when he was halfway down the steps.

"Sure, sure."

He opened the front gate just as Caden approached with a stride and a face stiffened with jealousy. It turned into a charming smile when Colin turned and Caden could see him. They shook hands. I went inside and closed the door but didn't lock it. When Caden came in, I was on the couch in my coat.

He locked the door. Looking at me, he tossed his keys onto the table. His beeper. His wallet. The bulge in his pants was distracting me, but not him. He was slow and deliberate, as if nothing could rush a man without feelings.

"I said naked," he said.

"Colin came to the door."

"Put your heels on the edge of the couch and spread your knees." He put his jacket on a hook and came to me, rolling up his sleeves.

I got my knees up, spreading them to show myself. His businesslike gaze had physical presence. He didn't just look between my legs; he stroked without even touching me.

"Naked is naked."

I shook off the coat. He undid his buckle, metal clicking on metal. Every cell in my body was drawn to him. Every inch of skin trembled for his touch.

I'd never seen him like this. He was as stone cold and far away as he'd ever been. I didn't know he could be this far inside himself.

And yet, he was still the guy in the stairway. The man who was afraid he would hurt me. The husband who risked everything for our marriage.

He looped the belt, holding the ends in his fist. "Don't flinch."

He tapped the loop of the belt in his palm, looking between my legs. My breath picked up, getting shallower and faster.

"What's naked?" he asked.

"Naked."

He slapped the inside of my thigh with the leather, and I flinched before it struck, then gritted my teeth from the raw sting, twisting with my knees together.

"Open your legs." He pulled them apart. "What are you afraid of?"

"You're going to hit my pussy with the belt."

He acted as if the thought had never occurred to him, raised the belt, and let it fall gently between my legs, sending sensation from my clit to my knees. The second tap was a little harder, and the third made me jump.

"You're afraid," he said, "and you're turned on."

"Yes."

"You think those two things might be related?"

A hard swipe fell inside my other thigh, leaving a burn behind.

I kept my legs open this time, daring him to do it again.

He smiled and bit his lower lip. "We do this thing every time. I hurt you or I control you, then I lose it for a second, and boom, I'm back to normal until I'm not anymore. Right?"

"Yes."

He reached his arm back, looking right at my cunt for aim, and I flinched. I flinched a lot. He put his arm down and smiled before he dropped the belt. He kneeled between my legs.

"What I thought today on the way here was, why do I rush to that middle part?" Then he pressed four fingers flat against his mouth and licked them. "Why? When you like getting hurt so much?"

He slapped his wet hand hard against my clit. It hurt so badly I lifted my bottom from the couch and screamed, but every sting, every jangling nerve blossomed into pleasure, and I gasped.

"You like it." He slapped again, and the pleasure bloomed bigger.

"I love it."

"What are you going to do when I feel too guilty to do this?"

The slap after was harder than the others, and I howled. He yanked my legs apart, and when I looked down, he had the belt again.

"No," I whispered.

"Come on, Grey. What's a limit if you can't push it?"

He hit me with the belt. The pain was extraordinary, exquisite, nearly unbearable, and so was the explosion of pleasure. I cried to God when he touched my raw clit, pinching it between two fingers. I was overstimulated and sore, overwhelmed with sensation.

Tight in his fingers, hood pulled back, he exposed my bare, red clit, pinching until the blood flowed to the rawest part. I got up on my elbows and locked eyes with him as he lowered his head and flicked it with his tongue.

My body expanded, taking up the entire room in electricity and heat, but I didn't explode. The detonator got warm but didn't blow.

"I think I knew the minute I met you." He gave me a tortuous lick. "I think I knew about you, but I didn't know about me." Still pinching, he flicked his nail on a raw membrane and thousands of nerve endings screamed in pain.

"I knew!" I cried, biting back a scream that would bring the police to the door. "About me."

He licked the bulb between his fingers. I was so close, yet he pulled away, leaving me on the edge. "Has it occurred to you I have no significant war trauma because my desire to hurt you is trauma enough?"

"No, that's not—"

Another flick and I writhed in pain.

"I can't. Caden, I can't take it."

"Yes, you can."

He put his lips around my clit and softly, gently, barely sucked on it. Then he let his fingers go. As the blood flowed back, expanding the capillaries and thrumming against the nerves, the pain grew explosive, but the pleasure of his mouth was just ahead of it, pulling the pain out to the brink of orgasm.

Then he stopped.

"Correlation," I said breathlessly. "Not cause."

He stood over me like a tower pushing up against the limits of the ceiling. "You're saying I'm not traumatized by my own needs, but that they just happen to correlate to this disaster of a marriage?"

Disaster of a marriage?

That was an ice-cold knife in my gut. Through everything, neither of us had labeled our union as anything but a buoy in a rough sea. The one stable, invariable thing through his ever-changing mental state.

I put my legs down. "What did you just say?"

"Don't worry about it. Really, Greyson. Tomorrow, I'll wake up in love again. Ready to conquer the world with my woman. Et cetera, et cetera." He put his hands on my knees and pressed them open slowly. I resisted. "But when you look at it objectively, and really, I'm the objective one here, this is a nightmare." He jerked my knees apart with more strength than I had to keep them closed. I fell back. "And you're feeding it."

He wedged himself between my open legs and pulled down his zipper.

230

"Are you angry?" In this state, he usually didn't feel anything. If he was angry, it was a step in the right direction.

"No." His cock was in his fist. "Not angry."

Seeking leverage in soft cushions, I tried to get up to a sitting position. "There's a name for this. For you."

"I've been called an asshole already."

"Not asshole. Something clinical."

"Really, baby?" He lined his cock along my entrance.

"Sadist."

"No, no. That's—"

"Your father. And you."

He thrust his cock into me, and I was torn between rage and the edge of climax. "I wasn't like this until you." He pushed so deep it hurt. So deep his body rubbed my raw, sensitive clit.

"You were too weak to see it." I looked deeply into the firmament behind his eyes. "Sadist."

He twisted me, pinning my right arm under my own weight and my left behind my back, fucking me as though he wanted to push through me. "You made this monster. How do you like it?"

Did I create this? Did he become what I wanted?

Did it matter?

"Sadist." I squeaked it one last time before his hands found my throat.

He bent me harder, pushing on my windpipe to growl in my ear. "Is this what you wanted?"

"Yes." I was choking.

"You like the monster I've become?"

"I love it." Barely a breath.

"I knew it." His fingers tightened.

I was handing him my life and my sex and my orgasm with both hands. I'd fantasized about this since I was a girl and finally... I had only a single breath to use to stop him.

"I love you," I croaked before he cut my air off completely.

In my last gasps, the orgasm detonated. Hot shrapnel pinged off the shell of my skin, stinging my armor from the inside, fighting for life, stiffening with pleasure as I looked into two holes punched through a rigid, red face, open to the blue Iraqi sky.

And black.

Chapter Twenty-Three

GREYSON

His face, briefly.

His lips on mine, briefly.

Then a breath like breathing charcoal.

Burn.

Breath again.

Cough.

Burn.

Darkness.

Cold.

Heave.

I got on my hands and knees, gulping air. Rolled to sitting. Shook out my bad wrist. No pain.

The lamp was still on, but the light in the sky was completely out. His clothes were all over the room—shirt on the coffee table, jacket over the fireplace grate—as if he'd stripped on fire.

If anything between Caden and I had ever been bad or dangerous, it didn't come close to what had just happened on the couch.

Was it the Blackthorne treatments? Were they stretching the time between episodes but making them more severe?

I got my coat on and clutched it closed against a coldness it couldn't protect me from. A chill from inside me. My feet were frigid against the wood. The front door was still locked. Between my legs, soreness and overuse hung like a weight. That had been the most intense sex I'd ever had. I didn't know if I'd live through it again.

"Caden?"

I flicked on the kitchen light. Empty.

Up the stairs. Lights still out. No sound.

"Caden!"

Office empty. Spare bedroom empty. Our room. Nothing.

I went back downstairs, continuing to the hall between my office and the back door.

Locked from the inside.

My eye caught the basement door. It wasn't closed all the way.

I opened it, and a waft of cold air hit me. I thought of running for shoes but decided to bear the cold, creaky steps.

Halfway down, shrouded in blackness, feeling the stone walls for the conduit to the light switch, I knew he was there. I couldn't see or hear him, but I knew.

"Caden?"

No answer, but I found the switch and clacked on the light. It flickered and steadied to a flat blue with a constant buzz.

Down to the dirt floor I crept, moving the false wall to the speakeasy and turning on the lights to illuminate the crumbling boxes and mosaic floor. I didn't waste time calling his name or looking in the corners. I knew where he was. The wall with the false vase was already half open. I made my way to the safe and opened it, turning on lights as I went.

The light right outside the safe was off. I flipped it on and opened the false wall in the back, crouching to get into the concrete room.

Caden was in the bottle room, huddled in the corner, naked and shivering. His beautiful body was rendered sexless in distress.

I rushed to him, dropping to my knees.

He didn't look at me.

Putting my hand on his cold skin, I squeezed his arm. "Hey."

His eyes were open and he was breathing evenly, but he didn't reply.

"Captain," I whispered, "it's cold."

He turned to face me. His eyes were the clear blue sky, his lips were full and soft, and his jaw was strong and square.

I knew that face, but I didn't.

But I did.

"I'm sorry," he said.

I knew that face in the moments before his release, in the sorrow of the man who'd wept in my arms after holding death and pain in his hands for eight straight days. This was the face I'd loved on my wedding day and in the broken hours of night.

I put my hands on that face and said his name.

"Damon."

TO BE CONTINUED

The Edge Series is four books.

Rough Edge | On The Edge | Broken Edge | Over the Edge

CHECK YOUR FAVORITE RETAILER FOR THE PREQUEL
—— CUTTING EDGE ——

FOLLOW ME ON FACEBOOK, Twitter, Instagram, Tumblr or Pinterest.

Join my fan groups on Facebook and Goodreads.

Get on the mailing list for deals, sales, new releases and bonus content - JOIN HERE.

My website is cdreiss.com

Also by CD Reiss

The Edge Series

Rough. Edgy. Sexy enough to melt your device.

Rough Edge | On The Edge | Broken Edge | Over the Edge

The Submission Series

Jonathan brings out Monica's natural submissive.

Submission | Domination | Connection

Corruption Series

Their passion will set the Los Angeles mafia on fire.

SPIN | RUIN | RULE

Affluence Series

Fiona has 72 hours to prove she isn't insane. Her therapist has to get through three days without falling for her.

KICK | USE | BREAK

Contemporary Romances

Hollywood and sports romances for the sweet and sexy romantic.

Shuttergirl | Hardball | Bombshell | Bodyguard